Readers love
ANDREW GREY

On Shaky Ground

"*On Shaky Ground* is a fast-paced, sexy office romance. As usual Andrew Grey created two great characters."

—TTC Book and More

"I cannot express how much I loved this book. It's such a sweet romance but so full of how people should be as well."

—Love Bytes

Fire and Obsidian

"This was such a great read. There is mystery and suspense. There is action and even some unlikely attraction. This is definitely one of my favorite books in this series so far."

—Gay Book Reviews

"This is a really well-written story, a wonderful combination of romance and suspense."

—Open Skye Book Reviews

Over and Back

"Thank you, Mr. Grey, for reuniting all the Boys so I could find out how they are doing because this series and the characters in it always held a special place in my heart."

—Paranormal Romance Guild

"I loved this story, it had everything in it: Lovable guys, a good plot, angst, emotional at times, and a satisfying end."

—Diverse Reader

More praise for
ANDREW GREY

Borrowed Heart

"Grey's breezy style makes it all go down smoothly. Fans of destination romances will find this one perfectly fits the bill."
—*Publishers Weekly*

"All in all, *Borrowed Heart* was a delightful mix of heavy-hitting personal issues and fluffy happily ever after story telling."
—Joyfully Jay

New Tricks

"I strongly suggest you get a copy, a cup of your favorite drink, a nice snuggly place to curl up and lose yourself in a wonderful world Andrew Greys making!"
—Love Bytes

"Another simply lovely heartwarming story by Andrew Grey."
—Open Skye Books

Reunited

"Sweet... it was a relaxing 20 minute read..."
—Gay Book Reviews

"Cute second chance at love story with a high school reunion turning into an unlikely first date."
—Open Skye Book Reviews

By ANDREW GREY

Published by DREAMSPINNER PRESS
www.dreamspinnerpress.com

Published by DREAMSPINNER PRESS
www.dreamspinnerpress.com

Twice Baked

ANDREW GREY

Published by
DREAMSPINNER PRESS

5032 Capital Circle SW, Suite 2, PMB# 279, Tallahassee, FL 32305-7886 USA
www.dreamspinnerpress.com

Twice Baked

Cover Art
http://www.tiferetdesign.com/
Cover content is for illustrative purposes only and any person depicted on the cover is a model.

Trade Paperback ISBN: 978-1-64405-592-2
Digital ISBN: 978-1-64405-591-5
Library of Congress Control Number: 2019903604
Trade Paperback published October 2019
v. 1.0

Printed in the United States of America

This paper meets the requirements of
ANSI/NISO Z39.48-1992 (Permanence of Paper).

To Lynne Perkin and all my fans.
Without each of you, I wouldn't be able to do what I love!

CHAPTER 1

IT ALL started with bananas. I can't believe it, but it's true. I hate the things with a *passion*, and I won't deny it. But what I can't fathom is that my life would turn on that hatred. See, I usually keep the foods I don't like a secret. When I dine with friends, I tend to keep quiet and eat the things I don't care for so I don't hurt anyone's feelings. I have become quite adept at cutting my food into small pieces and swallowing them whole so I don't have to taste it. But there are some things that I just cannot stand, like bananas—not even the smell of them.

Clare, my assistant, leaned over my shoulder. "Are you writing about them again? I know you hate them, but more on bananas? Just give it a rest, Luke." She smacked my arm.

"But it's the third anniversary of the blog, and I need to write something about the post that started it all." I knew what it was that my readers wanted to hear, and as long as I kept the post funny and a little irreverent, they would be pleased.

"Come on. You know I love you, but I still can't figure out how you can write a blog about the food you don't like and talk about restaurants that make a mess of everything, and become a huge internet sensation." She read from behind me. "You know, I think you should include pictures of all the banana stuff that people have sent you over the years. Show them that you got the gifts."

I liked that. "Go take the pictures for me, please. I'm going to finish this post, and we can include the pictures." I flashed her a smile, but Clare glared back. "Is there something else? You are my assistant, after all. Are you going to stand there and watch me write or actually assist me?"

She rolled her eyes. The truth was, Clare was a gem, and I was lucky to have her to help me. "I'll be off to do that." She set three slips next to my computer on the desk. "You can return these calls when you're done." She hurried away, closing the door to the back room of my home, which I used as an office.

I finished the written portion of the entry and then hit Save before letting my attention wander. I didn't want anything to happen to what I'd already written. Few things were more irritating than having to rewrite something.

Writing wasn't a skill that came naturally to me. It never had. The only reason I even started the blog was because I was so tired of hiding behind a mask of civility regarding the foods I don't like, and the blog gave me an outlet. What I didn't expect was to find so many people who either thought I was kidding or felt the exact same way.

I returned the first two calls, and was surprised to see the third was from an old friend from college. I hadn't heard from him in three or four years at least, but he and I had always had such a good time, so I called back right away.

"Justin," I said with delight. "How is the big television mogul?"

He snorted. "I'm just an assistant to the assistant of the mogul." Damn, it was good to hear his voice. "Beth asks about you all the time, and hopefully you'll be able to pay us a visit before the baby comes."

I swallowed. "Holy hell, you're going to be a father?" Now *that* was worth making a trip all the way across the country, even if the thought nearly made me ill. Airline travel always upset my stomach. I took enough medication just to get on the plane, and I always had to hope I didn't get sick anyway. If I was lucky, I just fell asleep. "I'll have to put it on my calendar. Maybe I can stay a few weeks to make it worth my while, but I really want to see you and Beth."

"Well…," Justin drew out. "I'm hoping I can entice you out here for a little longer than that. I have a new job working for the Cooking Network, and I know you're a fan because I read your blog. It's so hilarious, and I've learned so much about you, including why you were so thin all through college. Did you eat a danged thing the entire four years?" He laughed. "Anyway, we're mounting the next season of *Cooking Masters*, and we need a new guest judge. We bring someone new in each season to enliven the show and shake things up. This year we'd like you to be that judge. The network will fly you out and provide you a place to stay. We'll film fourteen episodes in about four weeks, once taping actually starts. There will be two weeks of preparation and rehearsal once the contracts are signed."

I was speechless, which was a situation I rarely found myself in. "You want me to judge a cooking competition?"

"Yes. You'll be fabulous, and you have a face and, if I might say so, a body for television. The ladies will all be drooling over your wavy blond hair, huge blue eyes, and your flawless complexion whenever you're on camera. They are going to absolutely love you, and I know you are going to have plenty of fans. And once you get used to being in front of the camera, I think you're going to be a natural."

I was more than a little shocked. "You're serious?"

"Yes. Absolutely. We would love to have you as part of our team for the season. Please think about it and let me know, but don't take too long. I need to have your answer in two days, and if you agree to come, then I'll make all the travel arrangements. Our producer has access to a private jet, so I believe I can arrange for you to come to Los Angeles in real style." He sounded so excited.

"Justin, I'm not qualified for something like that. I'm not a chef, and I don't have real cooking skills. I'm just a guy who snarks about the food he doesn't like." I really didn't understand where this was coming from, and I didn't want to make a fool of

3

myself week after week on television for everyone to see. But it was hard to turn down an opportunity like that.

"You know what you like, and you have a great way of expressing yourself. Besides, this is TV—you don't need to be a great chef to know good food. What works is personality, and you definitely have that. So stop worrying, think about it, and let me know right away. If you agree to do this, I need to get everything in motion."

I cleared my throat. "How many people have you already asked?"

Justin laughed. "I knew that question was coming. Believe it or not, you are the producers' first choice. They love your blog and think you'll make a great judge for the season."

It would be great to see Justin again, and as long as I got there in one piece, I'd be on the West Coast for a longer period of time, so I could get settled and relax between bouts of motion sickness. I really did hate to travel. Even in the car, I had to watch out the windows, no sleeping or reading, nothing to pass the time except listening to music or an audiobook, or otherwise lunch made a reappearance all over my shoes.

"I'll think about it, I promise, and I'll call you tomorrow."

"Great. Talk to you then," Justin said, then ended the call.

I looked up, counting to ten in my head. Clare burst in just as I finished counting. She was worse than the gossip in an old movie with a party line to listen in on.

"What cooking competition?"

"Did anyone ever tell you it's not nice to listen in?" I glared at her, but as usual, she ignored it. Clare was completely unashamed about her eavesdropping. She said it was because I was such a yutz that if she didn't keep an eye on me, I'd probably forget to eat and waste away to nothing.

"Yeah, you, at least once a week." She rolled her eyes. "Now spill."

What the hell? She knew most of it already. "That was Justin Marsh. He and I went to college together, and apparently the producers of *Cooking Masters* want me as their guest judge for the upcoming season."

She was speechless. Hell, I thought she might have fainted and forgotten to fall down. Clare was never silent, and she certainly wasn't still. Unfortunately, the quiet only lasted for about two seconds before she let out a scream that nearly broke my eardrums.

"Oh. My. God. You have got to do this. It's perfect for you." She hurried around to stand next to where I was sitting.

"What are you doing?"

"I'm about to push you out of the chair so I can write your acceptance letter and then get it sent off to this Justin Marsh before you have a chance to do something really stupid—like say no." She tilted her eyebrows as she scowled at me. "I've known you for two years, and you turn down chance after chance because you don't like to travel and get motion sick." Again with the major eye-rolling. "Just get over it, drug yourself up, and go. It will be a blast, and if it weren't for Maggie and Phillip, I'd finagle a way to go with you." Her expression softened, and she went back around the desk and sat in the comfy chair that she'd pretty much claimed as hers. "Why aren't you excited about this?"

"I am in a way. But what if I'm a total wet fish once they turn on the camera?"

Clare shook her head. "You're a little shy, I get that. But you have never been a wet fish. As soon as you pull yourself out of that hugely thick shell of yours, you shine. So just let it go, stop worrying, and do the show. Your followers love you, the site is doing amazingly well, and this is only going to stoke more interest, which is even better."

"I know," I whispered, even as my stomach did a little unsettled dance.

Clare leaned forward. "What's really the issue here? Does this have anything to do with Meyer Thibodeau?" The way she

5

said that name and the glazed look in her eyes was almost more than I could stand. Thankfully it only lasted long enough for me to start grinding my teeth. "It does. I still can't believe the two of you used to be together."

"I told you that in confidence, and you had better not be spreading it around." It was my turn to fix her with the scowl of death. "But yeah, I guess."

Three years ago, about the same time that I'd started the blog, Meyer had been an executive chef in Philadelphia. He and I had been dating for nearly two years at that point. I knew it was a disaster waiting to happen, because Meyer hadn't been willing to step out of the closet. The warning signs were there—I should have seen them. I really should have. Honestly, I can't even blame Meyer, because it was my own damn fault. I fell in love with him.

Meyer had been doing a regular spot on one of the local television channels, and he'd gotten a call from the Cooking Network to come out so they could talk to him. Since then, he'd been all over the network and had become a television celebrity as well as a restaurateur, with customers packing every table in his restaurants each night.

"Did he shatter your heart into little pieces?" Clare asked.

"No. I can't say that he did. I broke my own heart." I sighed. "It would be so easy to blame Meyer, but he had been up front with me about what he was willing to do and how far he was willing to go. It sucked, but I was the one who kept hoping he would change and realize I was there and would be there when he allowed himself to be true to who he was." I had been a fool of the highest order. "Then he got a call that was too good to pass up, and that was that. He was gone in a few weeks and went on to much bigger things and people than me." I tried not to admit it, but I thought about him sometimes. I'd be flipping channels and catch one of the shows he was hosting, and I couldn't help stopping just to watch him. Of course I didn't tell Clare that. She didn't have much time for "what could have been." That wasn't her thing, and I wished I could be more like her sometimes.

"That is the biggest bunch of bullshit I think I have ever heard in my life. A stand-up kind of guy would have broken it off. But I'm willing to bet that Meyer kept coming back to you even when you backed away." She sighed, and I couldn't deny it. "I know the type. I've dated plenty of losers in my life. The good ones are in hiding somewhere, or up in their apartments, blogging, and are gay."

I nodded. She pretty much had a handle on what had happened, all right. I had told myself that I wasn't going to be angry and bitter, but I hadn't meant to shift all the blame to me and internalize it. "Thanks," I said softly. Meyer was half a country away, and I could hate the guy if I wanted. Heck, if I ever saw him again, maybe a swift knee in his closeted nuts would be appropriate. Who knows?

"I don't get it. Are you afraid of stepping on his toes or something?" She shook her head once again.

"No. It's just that the whole television thing is his world, not mine." And I'd learned that it was best if I stayed in my own world. I could play there, even expand the boundaries, but making the jump to television wasn't something I thought I was willing to do. Even my thoughts were becoming convoluted, and I needed to figure things out for myself.

"So what? You have a presence and a gift all your own. There's no reason to be worried about him. It's been three years, and he made his choice. You need to make yours, and I think this is the right thing for you. Get out of your shell and wake up, have some fun. And if you end up shaking up his little world, then enjoy it, smile, and know you're evening the score. Besides, you're going to be a judge, which means you'll get to eat a whole lot of good food and tell people what you think about it. That's right up your alley. Be honest and have a good time. How long do they want you?"

ANDREW GREY

"I'll probably be out there six to eight weeks while they prepare and film the season."

"Then go. It isn't like they are going to want you to fly out tomorrow. Tell your friend that you'll do it, and then you can figure out all the other details. I'll be here to watch over things and make sure that Rosco is fed and gets some loving each and every day."

My cat—I had completely forgotten about him. He was my buddy and my companion. "I told Justin I'd think about it, and I will." That was the end of the story as far as I was concerned, at least for now. "Did you get those pictures?"

"Sure did." She smiled and handed me a memory stick.

I added the pictures of the stained glass window depicting a banana, and the banana squeaky toys and games that had been sent, and got the post uploaded. Within minutes there were a few comments from loyal followers, and I answered them before stepping away and letting the community take over. It was cool when the posts generated their own life and the comments went in their own direction. I tried not to interfere unless comments became rude, political, or just offensive. It was best to let things take their course.

"Is that it for the day?"

"I hope so. I already have tomorrow's post set and ready to go, and other than today, we're two weeks ahead, so it's all good unless something really unusual happens." I yawned and was already switching my attention over to work I had for clients.

Professionally, I was a graphic artist, and I had a small number of clients that I worked with. Each of the businesses had been very successful but didn't have the need for a full-time graphic artist on staff, so I fulfilled that role for them.

"Cool." She opened the door to leave. "I'll be at my apartment"—which was right downstairs—"if you need anything."

She breezed out, and Rosco poked his gray tiger head around the corner. He blinked, then pranced up to the desk and jumped on my lap before curling into a ball and starting to purr. I stroked his silky head for a few minutes and then got back to work, trying not to think about Justin's offer.

After a couple of hours, I was nearly caught up, and my mind decided now would be a good time to take a little trip to the internet. I told myself that I was going to check out past episodes of *Cooking Masters*. I had watched almost all the seasons, but seeing a few favorites would maybe help me figure out what I was going to do. But as soon as I clicked on the channel's website, there was Meyer, smiling out at me and the rest of the world. God, he was still gorgeous, with his mane of black hair that cascaded down to his shoulders and those dark eyes that called to me.

I knew this was a bad idea and life would be so much easier if I could be angry with the man. Hell, if I thought about it, maybe I was, and what I'd told Clare was just lip service. I mean, he'd moved to California, for Christ's sake. What was the big deal about coming out there? He could be himself, and I could work from anywhere. So why in the hell hadn't he asked me to join him? Maybe I wasn't good enough for him.

I closed the lid on the laptop, glad now to have banished his face. Screw him and his fear and ridiculousness. I couldn't believe that I was willing to stay away from a real opportunity just so I wouldn't accidentally run into him. That had to be the stupidest thing I had ever thought.

Rosco's motor ran loud, so while he purred and slept on my legs, I called Justin back.

"You're going to turn me down," Justin said.

"What? No. I'll do it." I needed to get the words out so I didn't change my mind. "Will you email me all the details of what I have to do and where I'll need to be? Oh, and I'm going to need to bring Rosco." He traveled fairly well, and at least I could have a little bit of home along with me. "By the way, are they going to pay me for this?" I probably should have asked earlier.

"Yeah. It's a hundred thousand for the entire season. So this will be worth your while. It's just a flat appearance fee. No residuals or things like that."

I wasn't going to complain about that kind of money for a couple months' work.

"Let me send you the schedule and all the details. I'll have the producers' office send over a contract. Get your lawyer to look it over, sign it, and get it back to us so we can finalize everything and get you out. Things move a little fast around here, and I'm thrilled that we're going to get to see you." I thought he was going to hang up, but he paused. "By the way, who is Rosco?"

"My cat. He'll be coming with me." I stroked Rosco's head, and he purred louder, lifting his head to blink at me. "That's right, you're going to come with me."

Justin chuckled. "Okay. That shouldn't be a problem. I can arrange for that too. Talk to you soon." And just like that, Justin was gone.

My email indicated that I had a message, and then another. I read over the emails, and everything looked pretty good to me. I forwarded them to Vince, my lawyer, who messaged that everything was good. So I signaled that I was ready to move forward. Maybe this could be fun after all.

CHAPTER 2

MAN, WHEN Justin said things moved fast, he wasn't kidding.

The next day I had a contract that I forwarded to Vince to review, and as soon as it was signed, Justin made housing and travel arrangements, and I was on my way. Clare was watching the house for me as Rosco and I sat in first class—no private jet—for a flight across the country.

I was doped to the gills and slept most of the way. I didn't dare eat, which was fine with me. One tray contained something smothered in gravy, and one look was enough to put me off what little appetite I might have had. Rosco slept in his carrier near my feet, positioned so he could see me. He whined to be let out a few times, but with a couple of cat treats and some attention, he settled down again.

By the time we landed in Los Angeles, the pills had started to wear off, but the landing was smooth. Rosco and I were off the plane and the queasy feeling passed. A driver met us in baggage claim, loaded the luggage into the car, and we were off to the new apartment.

"Is this your first time in Los Angeles?"

"No. I was here a few years ago, but only for a few days." That trip had been hell on so many levels. I had foolishly come out to see Meyer, and the flight and the visit had been awful. I ended up staying three days and went home, arriving dehydrated and completely wrung out. "I like it here, but I haven't had a chance to see very much of the city." Maybe this time I would be able to rectify that.

"I can take you anywhere you'd like to go. The studio has arranged for me to be your driver during your stay." He turned and flashed me a smile when we stopped at the traffic signal before the entrance ramp for the freeway. I didn't remember that in the agreement, but I was more than grateful. Living in the city, I didn't drive much and had been expecting to give Uber and Lyft a great deal of money in order to get around.

"That's very nice. Thank you. Right now, I need to get to where I'll be staying so I can rest." I had a meeting in the morning and was going to need to not look like complete hell when I walked in or else they were going to wonder why they'd hired me.

"No problem." He turned back around, and the car slid forward.

I tried to relax, watching out the window and soothing Rosco, who was getting impatient to be out of the carrier.

My home of the next couple of months was a small apartment in Glendale. It was on the twentieth floor of a new, rather dull-looking building, but the view of the hills was stunning. I let Rosco out of his carrier as soon as I had closed the door. I unpacked his things, got him some water and food, and set up his litter box in the bathroom, showing him where it was, then collapsed onto the beautifully made-up bed.

I woke a few hours later to knocking on the door. Rosco complained as he got off the bed to follow me. I was careful not to let him outside as I opened the door. Justin stood with a huge fruit basket and two recyclable grocery bags.

"I brought you some provisions, and this is from the producers—no bananas." It seemed he had indeed read my blog.

"Thanks." I motioned him inside, and he set the things on the glass coffee table and drew me into a hug.

"It's good to see you."

"You too. How is Beth doing?"

"Really well. She isn't due for another four months, so she intends to keep working for a little while longer." He stepped back. Justin looked good, with sun-kissed skin, lighter hair than he'd had in college, trim figure, a huge smile on his lips. "Things are working out for us. She and I are thinking of looking at houses, but they are so expensive out here that it's probably going to take us a little while longer before we can afford it."

We wandered over to the windows to look out, and Rosco wound around my legs until I picked him up. He got a good look out the windows and instantly wanted down, the height probably freaking him out. "So what is the plan?"

"Tomorrow you have a meeting. It's just a meet and greet, but this way you can be introduced to everyone on the show, including the producers, other judges, and the staff. We all work together to make the show great, and what you see on television takes a lot of time in the studio and editing room to put together. Have you unpacked?"

"Not really. I was sleeping when you knocked. The time difference and all." I didn't go into the whole travel-sickness thing. It wasn't necessary.

"Good. What did you bring?"

"Just clothes," I answered, and Justin groaned.

"Then we need to go shopping. You are going to need clothes to make you look good on television. What are your sizes?" he asked, and I rattled off pants and shirt sizes, along with the size of the suit coat in my luggage. Justin got right on the phone, and soon he was talking to someone, ordering shirts, pants, jackets, and ties, relaying my sizes. "Shoes?"

"Have to try them on. It varies."

Justin hung up. "Our personal shopper is gathering a number of things for you to try on. We'll need to go down to check the fits, and then everything can be delivered to the set, so the clothes will be washed and pressed for when we're taping. Once you've worn them, just take them with you, because we won't reuse outfits." He sat on the sofa, and I used the chair.

"I take it you like it out here," I said.

"Beth was born in Pasadena, so this is her home and I doubt she'll ever want to leave. I like it here too. The weather is hard to

13

beat, and the work is awesome. I know you're doing the blog thing, but that can't be all."

"Nope. The blog started out as something for fun, and it's grown all on its own. Once I was able to monetize it, it turned into a nice little side business, but my main job is as a graphic artist. My neighbor, Clare, helps me out, and so does Rosco here. He sits on my lap and keeps me company as I work." Rosco had curled up on one side of the sofa, basking in a ray of light that came through the side window.

Justin's phone chimed, and he checked the message. "We should go. The clothes are ready, and that's something we can tick off the list. You'll be able to wear some of them tomorrow, so the producers will be able to see how you'll look."

I figured I might as well get the full Hollywood treatment, and once we were downstairs, the car I'd arrived in pulled up in front and carried us off to a huge mall department store. Justin walked inside, barely looking at anything on display, and went right to the elevators, where we were whisked upward to the domain of the personal shopper.

THE FOLLOWING morning when the car arrived, I was ready and downstairs. We glided down city streets, past a gate, and onto one of the studio lots, barely stopping until we reached a large building that had *Cooking Masters* emblazoned on the side in their signature logo.

"Good luck," the driver said.

"Thank you… I don't know your name," I said.

"Felix," he answered, and I smiled, reaching in to shake his hand.

"It's good to know you. Should I text when I need you to come back?"

He shook his head. "I'll be right here waiting for you. Just come on out. I have a good book and plenty of water and coffee."

I smiled and girded my loins as I reached the soundstage door and went inside. A number of people were busily preparing the set and moving things around, jumping at the instructions of the man in charge. It looked like controlled chaos to me, but then, it probably was.

On television, the set looked really polished, like it was placed in the kitchen of a fine restaurant, but all of that was an illusion. It was a set, and behind it were walls of a tall soundstage. As I thought about it more, the entire idea was pretty impressive.

"Luke," Justin called as he approached, the whir of power tools covering up much of what he'd said.

"This is something. Do they rebuild the set like this for every season?"

"No. Most of it is stored away and reassembled, but after last season, it was looking a little shabby, so the producers decided on a redesign of the set in order to add some freshness. We also learn what works after each season and try to incorporate improvements for the next one." He motioned, and I followed him off the set and through a side door, back out into the California sun. We crossed the area between buildings and entered a much smaller one that resembled a house of sorts. The reception area was filled with people, and I was introduced to the crew, director, and the producers.

"We're so glad to have you on board," one producer said as he shook my hand, then almost immediately turned to the man next to him in earnest conversation.

I glanced at Justin, who didn't seem to notice as we made our way through to a small conference room. I took my seat next to Rachel Graham, and smiled. I'd seen her on other cooking shows. She was a regular judge and expert, and I was a little starstruck.

"Luke Walker," I said, holding out my hand. "It's nice to meet you, Rachel."

She smiled, probably at being recognized. "I love your blog," she told me, and I grinned. "It's funny and snarky, and I love how unabashedly honest you are about the fact that not everybody loves everything. We do these shows sometimes with strange ingredients and make them sound so normal."

"I know. Sometimes the ingredients seem so unappetizing. I was worried when they approached me, because trying to force down things I don't like is getting harder and harder for me." Since I'd opened up about it on the blog, it had become even more difficult.

"The chefs on this show usually make really good food, and it's a joy to eat it. I'm sure it's going to be an amazing experience." She shifted her chair to look at me better. "I know you're a little nervous, but you're going to do fine. This is my fourth season on the show, and I was nervous when I started. Just be yourself and have fun with it. That's what viewers want to see." She patted my hand gently, leaning closer. "And don't let the Hollywood types get to you. They're always looking really busy because they think it makes them seem important." She rolled her eyes and flashed a gorgeous, warm smile.

"That's good to know." I smiled back and tried not to fidget too much.

"Please. I'm a girl from outside Butte, Montana. I know the real world beyond these soundstages, sets, and makeup. People love this show because it's a competition and because they're sitting at home, watching chefs cook, looking at the food and thinking that they might like to eat this dish or that dish. Our job is to either confirm their thoughts or burst their bubble. Either way, we give them the truth as we see it, and then we get together and choose the best dish." She leaned close once again. "I will admit that there are times when I want to spit the food out and make a yuck face like I did when I was a kid."

"Oh, thank God," I whispered, because there had been times when I'd done that just watching the television. I chuckled, and she laughed softly but with genuine feeling. I was beginning to really like her.

Others began filing in, and Rachel returned her chair to face the table. Everyone took a seat, with the place next to me remaining empty.

"Where is he?" one of the producers—I think his name was Claude—said, and an assistant standing behind him ran out of the room like it was on fire.

"We'll get started in just a minute, but it's good to have you both with us," Claude said, folding his hands on the table. He must have been the lead producer, because no one else made an effort to speak, even when he grew quiet. "This is our eighth season, and we wanted to do a few things to shake it up." The assistant returned, whispered something in Claude's ear, and then stepped back. "It seems our final judge was caught in traffic, but he's just passed through the gate." He spoke softly with the man next to him, and then the door opened.

My heart fluttered for a second as Meyer strode through the door. He looked as fantastic as he always had, with that incredible long hair and those amazing eyes.

Then it hit me—*Meyer* was who we were waiting for.

I forced myself to remain sitting upright in my chair as he looked around the room. I knew the instant he spotted me. I suppressed a smile as he paled slightly, then walked to the seat next to me and sat.

"What are you doing here?" he whispered.

"I'm a judge this season," I answered, and grew quiet as Claude got everyone's attention.

"I want to keep this meeting brief because we all have work to do, but I'm pleased to introduce all of you to our judges for season eight of *Cooking Masters*. Rachel Green is returning as our host, and Meyer Thibodeau is joining us as our head judge for the season. I'm sure you are familiar with his other work on the network. Food blogger Luke Walker will be stepping in as our third, seasonal guest judge." He cleared his throat and paused for a second, probably for dramatic effect. "Meyer has quite a following on the network, and we believe he is going to do an amazing job for us. We have worked with Rachel before, and I know she will bring her sense of style and pizzazz to the show. So it is going to be a great season."

I didn't take offense at not being mentioned again. The others had real cred on the show, and I was an unknown.

The doors opened, and a young lady wheeled in a cart with coffee and water. The meeting paused as people moved about to get drinks.

"You're a judge?" Meyer growled under his breath. "I didn't think that would be something you're qualified for."

What a snarky ass.

"Yeah, and you're going to have to put up with me for the next two months," I retorted, then winked at him, putting on my most mischievous "I know a secret" grin. Two could play that game. "I think it's going to be so much fun seeing how you work."

Meyer paled.

"Do you two know each other?" Rachel asked.

"Yes," I answered. "Meyer and I—"

"Knew each other in Philadelphia before I relocated to Los Angeles."

I noticed he left out the part about it being in the biblical sense. The crack in Meyer's composure lasted only a few seconds, and then it was gone, the wall of his facade concreted and whole once again. Not that I had any intention of telling anyone anything that Meyer didn't want known. He and I had a past that Meyer still seemed desperate to keep under wraps. I didn't know why, but the reasons were his, and I was never going to out anyone, for any reason. Yes, if I was honest, the closet case had hurt me pretty badly, but his secrets were still his to tell. The way someone came out and grew to be honest with themselves was their business, and I wasn't going to take that from anyone. Dante had a certain level of hell reserved for those who were that despicable.

"Meyer and I were friends some time ago, but we lost touch, and I don't think he was expecting to see me here. Right, Meyer? It was a surprise to both of us." I gave him a friendly, guy shoulder bump. He stiffened, and I could tell he was trying not to overreact. Lord, the man was as uptight as anyone I had ever met.

"As I was saying." Claude drew everyone's attention back to him, getting control of the meeting once again. "The episodes will largely be filmed here on the set, but we have arranged for two of them to be filmed in two of Meyer's restaurants. Those location shoots will be done on Mondays, when they are closed, and are noted in the filming schedules. One episode will be filmed outdoors with cooking over open fires or something along that line, and we have secured a private location for that. The remainder of the episodes will be filmed here on the set under various circumstances, and a number of them will be built around Mr. Walker's blog."

I swallowed. "Excuse me?" I said. This was the first I'd heard of it.

Claude seemed surprised. "Since you agreed to judge, we thought that we would build some episodes around you. As an example, one of our signature challenges will feature bananas, and the chefs will need to make a dish that they think will change your mind about them. There will be four such challenges throughout the season, and we have picked the ingredients you seem to hate the most: bananas, mushrooms, salmon, and gravy."

I couldn't help making the yuck face and shivering in disgust. The thought of eating God knows how many dishes with those components nearly overwhelmed my system. I could almost feel my taste buds rolling over to play dead, and I swallowed hard as I tried to keep from gagging. Just the banana episode was going to be death on a plate, let alone the rest.

"That's perfect," Claude said. "I love that face. You feel free to make it any time you don't like something. We'll build some of the promo around it, and everyone is going to tune in to see what could taste so bad."

"Good God," Meyer mumbled, "you haven't changed a bit. I thought your taste buds would grow up at some point."

I glanced around the table and saw that everyone had heard. "And I figured you might have learned that not everyone is exactly like you. If they were, then the world would be up to its ears in jackass." I plastered on a smile and dared Meyer to one-up me. Instead, he blushed. God, I really loved to win. "I'm so sorry, Claude. Please continue."

He said nothing about the little drama, but I could have sworn dollar signs flashed behind his eyes. I'd seen enough competition shows to know that drama was worth its weight in gold. And, hell, if Meyer wanted to be snarky, then I could meet him snark for snark, and let the better snarker win.

"We are finalizing the shooting schedule now and the set is still being built, but we'd like to run through a few mock episodes tomorrow in order to make everyone familiar with the format, what to expect, and so that everyone can get used to the cameras." He looked right at me when he said that last part, and I nodded. "Are there any questions?" Which everyone else seemed to take as "you better not have any, and if you do, ask them privately," because it was the only time the room was quiet.

I raised my hand anyway. "What are shooting days like? What time should I plan to be here?"

Claude nodded. "Good question. We will post a detailed schedule each day with set call times, which means you need to be here two hours earlier for makeup, wardrobe, and other prep. The days are long—I won't sugarcoat it. You will have a trailer where you can rest when you aren't needed on set. If you have any other detail questions, Justin can provide any information you need. But…." Claude looked around the room and got very serious. "Things go wrong, we know that. They always do. Days get longer, and some challenges will have unusual start times. I expect everyone to pull their weight and do their part to make this season as successful as the others." He stood to indicate that the meeting was over, and everyone began filing out of the room.

"I bet there's a story between the two of you," Rachel said with a glint in her eye.

I said nothing to confirm as Meyer grew tense enough to fly apart. "Meyer and I had a difference of opinion before he left Philadelphia. That's all. He and I left a lot of things unsaid, and I think they festered for longer than either of us realized." I stood and followed the others out to where Justin waited for me.

"That was interesting," Justin said with a wink. My friend was fully aware that I was gay. I hadn't hidden it while I was in college, which was a point of contention with Meyer—just one of what turned out to be many.

"We don't gossip, do we?" I asked Justin, and his eyes widened.

He shook his head. "I know more secrets than anyone else realizes. That's part of how you get ahead here. Keep your mouth shut, look, listen, and compile as much knowledge as you can." The part about using it at the appropriate time was left unsaid, but I got the idea.

"How very Machiavellian of you," I countered, with a smile of my own. I had the idea that my visit was going to be fun, but when the show was over, I was going to be more than ready to leave this land of make-believe and intrigue to go back home.

"It's survival." Justin led the way out. "Let's go over to the set so I can familiarize you with how things flow and where you'll be spending a lot of your time."

"Aren't we going to get in the way?" I asked as I followed.

"No. I already informed the crew that we were coming over. They are working to finish up the kitchen settings. We're going to spend time in the judging studio." He pulled open the door. There was just as much activity going on as there had been before, but Justin walked around the edge, staying out of the work area, and then we entered a back area with a large desk surrounded by stainless-steel panels broken up by lattice. It looked like a very sleek restaurant without the tables.

"This is awesome," I said, glancing around.

"Your place is right on the end here. Meyer will sit next to you, then Rachel, and the last seat is for the weekly guest chef," Justin said, motioning as he spoke.

I walked behind the desk and took a seat on one of the padded high-seated chairs. "It seems low." Actually, I felt like I was a kid at the grown-up table. Hell, maybe I was.

"Don't worry, they'll be adjusted for each of you so all four people are the same height." Justin stood in front of the desk. "The chef contestants will be standing there. The lighting will be dramatic, and you'll talk to them."

"Is each of us miked?" That was going to take some getting used to.

"In some cases, yes. But in here, the room will be set up so we can turn off various areas to minimize background noise. We use boom microphones, and if you look up, you'll see them in the ceiling. They get lowered when they're needed, then turned off and retracted so only the areas we wish to hear will make it to tape."

"Well, look at little Luke, sitting at the table with the big boys," Meyer said as he strolled in, barely giving Justin a second look.

"Who are you, the big man on campus?" I grinned. "You know, I really do know the kind of man you are." I held Meyer's gaze hard for a few seconds. "You certainly can be an ass when you want. That hasn't changed."

He didn't pause as he approached the desk. "You're actually going to do this?"

I chuckled. "I'm already contracted. Signed, sealed, and here I am." I leaned over the desk. "Why don't you cut the crap and act like a real person instead of this fake asshole you seem to have become." I knew what I had seen in him—then. But I was starting to wonder if there was anything of that man left. At one time Meyer had been attentive and kind, at least when we were

22

alone. He used to smile in a way that could warm you through, and when he did, one gaze was enough to speed up my heart until I swore it beat loudly enough for the entire world to hear. "You used to be decent." I stood and slowly walked back around the desk to Justin. "I think I've seen what I need to here. I assume that I'm not just going to be in this area?" Meyer excused himself and left, checking his phone.

"No. You and Rachel will host some of the appetizer rounds, and those generally get judged in the kitchen area. I'm sure they'll take you through those in the mock-ups so you can get used to how the cameras follow you."

I nodded, wondering what I was going to do to get the hang of this. "I'm not a television personality. What if I screw this up?"

"The biggest thing is for you to just be yourself. The camera operators are pros and will get the best angles. You speak to the contestants, and they'll capture it." Justin turned to me, as serious as a heart attack. "You can do anything you choose to. Remember senior year? You didn't know anything about sports and didn't play, but when they threatened to cut intramurals because of the cost, you fought it as hard as any of us because you thought it was important that sports be open to everyone, not just the people on the teams, and you joined a baseball team just to make your point."

I laughed. "Yeah, and I sucked so badly, and my team ended up in last place."

"True, but we all had fun, and the college relented and kept the sports program. That was the real goal, not for you to learn baseball. This"—Justin motioned around us—"isn't baseball. It's more like the fight. Be passionate and yourself, and it will come through to the viewers."

The workmen were still bustling around the set, so Justin took me out without stopping and we got into the car.

"Can we get lunch? I'd prefer a salad or something light, and then if I'm not needed, I'd like to go back to the apartment."

"Sure." Justin's phone dinged, and he tapped and studied it while the car moved forward, eventually turned around, and passed through the gates. "I got your schedule, and they believe they will have the set ready in two days. They have the first walk-through scheduled for Thursday, with members of the crew standing in as chefs."

"Good. Then I have a few days to get some other work done and try to get over this time change." It was only three hours, but just enough to kick my butt, especially in the morning.

"Yes. Use the car for the next few days. The driver will give you his number." Justin slid closer in the back seat, and I flashed him a warning look in case he was getting too familiar, then turned to watch out the windows as street upon street of low-rise buildings passed outside for as far as the eye could see. "Tell me, what is it with you and Meyer? Is it going to affect the show?"

"I doubt it. Meyer and I will figure things out eventually. We have to work together, and Meyer is many things, but he isn't about to shoot himself in the foot and damage his professional reputation. He has too much riding on it." I sighed and tried not to think about him.

Once we reached the building after stopping for a light lunch, I got out of the car, thanked Felix, and went inside and up to the apartment, where Rosco greeted me by rubbing my legs and meowing to let me know he missed me—or probably because he was hungry. I fed and watered him, then sat at my computer to try to work.

I didn't. As soon as I woke up my laptop, I searched for information on Meyer. I found the usual entertainment articles and things, stuff I already knew. But as I continued down the list, I wondered about a page from a children's cancer charity. I clicked on it, and there was Meyer smiling at the top of the article, surrounded by kids in one of his restaurants. As I continued, I found more articles and stories. It seemed Meyer did a lot of work with charities. There were dinners at various restaurants, banquets, and other events where he was a guest chef, donating his name and talent for the benefit of others.

I had always known that somewhere deep down was a good person. That had been part of why I'd stayed around for so long, I guess. At least Hollywood hadn't changed him so completely. That was good to know.

I stared at a picture of Meyer in his chef whites behind a table, grinning as he did what he did best—cook up a storm.

I closed the browser as Rosco jumped on my lap. "Yeah, I know. It's time to go to work." Rosco made himself comfortable, and I sat back to try to get something accomplished, but my thoughts kept wandering.

CHAPTER 3

"Do they want me in makeup?" I asked once I located Justin standing off to the side of the set the following Thursday.

"Not today. Though after the rehearsals, we'll take you over so they can figure out what's best to do. When you're in the kitchen, you'll have minimal stuff on because of the steam and things. But when you're judging, the makeup folks will have you looking your television best." Justin motioned toward the set, which was all laid out with stainless-steel worktables, ovens, stoves, pantries, and racks of dishes and pans. It was quite impressive.

"Everyone," the director said as he came over. "Ethan Kilgard," he said with a genuine smile as he shook my hand. "It's great to meet you. I'm sorry I couldn't earlier, but I had to supervise. You're Luke Walker. I love your blog." He leaned closer. "And I hate bananas as much as you do."

A kindred spirit of sorts. "Thank you."

"Rachel and Meyer, let's go over this," Ethan said, and they came over. "We aren't going to be cooking anything today, but the crew is going to stand in for the contestants. They'll present their plates, and I want Rachel and Luke to pretend to taste them and then react. Go from station to station, talk, chat, taste, and move on. Crew, you have descriptions of your dishes, so present them like you're proud of them, and we'll just run through it. We will be taping, but only so we can get Luke used to the camera. Okay... let's go. Action."

"As a reminder, each chef was to make their signature mushroom appetizer," Rachel said, as though she was on the show. "What do you have for us, Julio?"

26

Julio smirked. "Grilled portobello mushrooms with lemon and caper crème, over cauliflower puree," he said, and damned if my throat didn't threaten to seize up.

Rachel pretend tasted, and then I did.

"It tastes a little salty to me," she said as she considered the dish.

I tried to come up with something insightful that would roll off my tongue, and stumbled.

"It's okay, Luke. Think of the dish and what you think it would taste like," Ethan prompted.

"Be yourself," Justin said from the wings.

I took another pretend taste. "Tastes like dirt with cream sauce over a mushy puree of battery acid," I blurted in my nervousness.

The others snickered, and even Rachel covered her mouth.

"For God's sake," Meyer interrupted loudly. "You need to act like you know what the hell you're doing. You can't even fake it during rehearsal. How are you going to eat the real food?" I didn't need to see Meyer to know he was probably shaking his head and rolling his eyes halfway to the ceiling. I was well acquainted with that look.

"That was perfect," Ethan said. "An honest reaction. It's just what we want. Luke, lay it on as thick as you want. Say what you think, just like in the blog. Now, don't use up your best quips in rehearsal. Save it for the real show." He could barely contain his glee.

"Oh my God. This is going to be a circus," Meyer groaned.

"And who will be the gorilla?" I said over my shoulder.

Rachel and I continued down the line, repeating the process at each station. Then we stepped back to a small piece of tape on the floor to deliberate.

"If you make those quips during the show, I'm going to have to bite my tongue to keep from laughing," Rachel whispered as we pretended to think about what we had just eaten.

"Challenge accepted," I retorted, and then we turned to the camera, facing forward.

"Luke, will you announce the winner?"

"The contestant whose dish made me least likely to gag is… Rodney." I was getting into it now, and Rachel doubled over with laughter as Rodney put his hands in the air in celebration of his mock win.

"Ethan, you can't be serious," Meyer said. "This is really what you want?"

"From him, yes. Viewers thought the last few seasons were too stuffy. He's going to bring some humor and lightheartedness to the show. You and Rachel are to play it straight. Luke, don't go overboard, but keep it real, and the viewers are going to love you. Most of the time, you should keep a straight face and be serious, but every now and then, let it fly. It will have more impact. Now, I want to run it again, this time quicker. This should take only a few minutes. We'll edit out any mistakes and fumbles, but we need to keep the show moving."

We repeated the exercise, and it went more smoothly. I stopped paying attention to where the camera was every second and interacted with the contestants and Rachel. I kept it businesslike and did my best to learn.

"That was great. Very natural and real. You looked good, Rachel. Now, let's run through a final judging." Ethan moved everything to the other area, the crew took their places as contestants, and we went through the final process a couple of times. I was acutely conscious of Meyer, so I was quieter with him right next to me. We were talking things over, and I knew that in a real show, a lot of what we said would be cut in order to try to hide who we thought the winner was until the actual announcement was made.

Rachel asked our absent guest to announce the winner, and then she told the loser that their kitchen was closed. I had seen the show enough that this part was quite easy.

"Luke, don't be nervous. And you need to talk more. Let Rachel guide the conversation so you don't talk over each other, but when your time comes, you need to express your opinion. Say what you like and what you don't. And remember, you have just as much say as Meyer, Rachel, and our guest judge."

"Okay. I'll try," I said, and Ethan had us run through the exercise again.

"THIS IS going to be a shitshow," Meyer said into his phone. I knew he was referring to me, and it pissed me off. I sat in one of the makeup chairs, where they were trying various things to get the look right.

"Excuse me," I said softly, and got up out of the chair. Meyer had his back to me, so I guess he thought that meant his voice wouldn't carry. The makeup robe fluttered over my clothes as I approached. Meyer must have heard me coming, because he turned just in time for me to snatch his cell phone and disconnect the call. "If you have a problem, you talk about it. Don't act like some little weasel on the goddamned phone, whining like a little baby." *That* I was sure everyone heard. Then I stepped close enough that only Meyer could hear. "Let go of the fear. I'm not going to say anything or betray your privacy. But you need to stop acting like the biggest dick on the face of the earth." I stepped back again. "And for God's sakes, stop taking yourself and everything else so seriously, or else that stick you have lodged halfway up your ass is going to break off." I turned, went back to my makeup chair, and sat back down as though nothing had happened.

Meyer stared at me, his lower lip and jaw working. I knew he was grinding his expensive dental work, but the guy needed to lighten up. He was way too serious.

"What would you have made for that appetizer challenge?" I knew him well enough to know that giving him something else to talk about might ease the tension.

"Something with mushrooms so you might like it?" He shook his head. "There is nothing that anyone can do to make mushrooms palatable for you. They're in that category of things that you can taste from a mile away and can't stand."

"Yup…." I met his gaze.

"The only time you willingly ate them was on a pizza once, when they were cut really small and it was too difficult to pick them off. And even then you said they made the pizza taste dirty." Finally Meyer laughed. "You never liked the things in any way. But if I were to try, I'd use plenty of garlic and other flavorings to mask the 'dirt' flavor you hate. The other judges might criticize it, but it would be the one dish you would be most likely to eat."

I nodded slowly. "Possibly," I agreed. "But I don't know how this is going to work. I haven't made any bones about the things I don't like. I've put them out there, boldly forward for the world to see." It occurred to me that it wasn't the humor or the snark that was bothering Meyer, but the fact that maybe I was garnering the attention. I kept that little tidbit to myself. Meyer was going to have to learn that the sun couldn't always shine on him.

"The others are right," Meyer said flatly. "You need to be yourself. That's the only way this is going to work. If you do anything else, it will come across as fake, and that is the kiss of death. Hollywood is fake—it's plywood sets with nothing behind them, but it has to look real and feel real, even if it isn't." He sighed slightly, his expression darkening for a second, and then, without another word, he turned on his heel and strode toward the exit. The conflict in his eyes left me wondering at the true source even after he'd gone.

I had no idea if I had just been offered some sort of peace deal or what.

"Don't worry," the makeup woman, Darlene, said. She had been quiet for the entire exchange, continuing to check shades against my cheeks. "This is Hollywood, the land of big egos and people who wish they had what you have."

30

I turned to her. "Excuse me?"

"Sweetheart," Darlene said gently. "You have that presence. Turn to the mirror. Those eyes and that mouth—you have a face that, once I'm done with it, is going to stop traffic. You're funny and you stand up for yourself. That's a pretty powerful combination. And that is going to frighten some people." She wagged her pinkie, and I snorted, trying not to laugh. She could wave that pinkie all she wanted, but if she was referring to Meyer, then she was way off in that department. I went along with her joke and did my best not to give away any indication that I knew something to the contrary.

"I've never had any sort of presence in my life. I'm the guy that everyone overlooks." It had always been that way.

Darlene patted my shoulder through the cape. "You need to spend a little more time seeing what's really there, rather than in your head. This is Hollywood, where everything is only skin-deep. Beautiful people in movies and on television. You're interesting and have personality, but you're also good-looking and your face has real character. It's not plastic or cookie-cutter-looking. All you need to do is learn to use it." She finished up and stepped away. "Take a look and tell me what you think."

I turned toward the mirror and widened my eyes. It was hard to believe that it was me staring out of the mirror. "Good God, what did you do?"

"I evened out your skin tone some, and highlighted your eyes just enough to make them appear a little larger. Most of that is to counter the effects of the cameras. Otherwise, it's all you." She smiled as I grinned, looking at myself anew. "I'm going to make some notes so I can do this each morning that we're filming, and you'll be good to go."

"Do you come along when we go on location too?"

"Yup. I'm your best makeup friend." She smiled and patted my shoulder once more. "Just be yourself and remember to smile with your eyes."

31

I couldn't help chuckling at the *America's Next Top Model* reference. "I'll do my best."

She took away the cape and handed me a tissue and some cream. "Use this to remove the makeup, and be sure to wash your face thoroughly at the end of the day. You want to make sure your pores remain open and clear. Otherwise you'll get blemishes, and that isn't going to be good. Now, I think wardrobe is waiting for you." She shooed me off, and I thanked her for everything.

I headed over to the wardrobe area, where the clothes that Justin had arranged for me hung on racks. He and I went over what they thought I would wear for each episode and marked them. He explained that, other than some shirts and basic pants, the rest couldn't be worn more than once, and he confirmed that I would be given them once they were finished.

"You certainly can wear clothes," the man said, looking me over. "Some people are so bulky, it's hard to get things to fit."

"Well, thank you," I said as he fussed a few moments. "Is there anything I need to do to help you?"

"Yes, try not to slobber down yourself. We had a judge two seasons ago who wore more food than he ate, and we ended up buying two of everything so we could have something to change him into." He rolled his eyes. "I trust you'll be more careful."

"I'm not a messy eater, just a picky one." I met the older man's gaze. He hadn't bothered to introduce himself.

"That's a good one, kid," he said, and actually started to smile. "Okay. You come here after makeup, and we'll get you dressed and ready for the show. Sometimes we'll have you change between the filming of the challenges and the judging, and sometimes you'll just put on a jacket. We want you to look nice at all times."

"I understand. So, I can arrive in casual clothes?" I was hoping there wasn't some in-studio dress code.

"I'd keep changes in your dressing room. That way you have options." He sat down on a stool and reached for a sandwich out of a cooler bag.

"How long have you been doing this?" I asked as I got ready to leave.

"I've been with this show every season, and I work on a lot of others too. I've worked at the studio about thirty years. I've dressed some really big stars. You know, the bigger they are, the nicer they are. It's the ones who think they're really something who are the biggest pain in the rump." He flashed a smile and took a bite.

"You have a good day, and I'll be seeing you." I pulled open the door and stepped out in the late-day sun. It was still intense, but waning, with the shadows growing longer. As far as I knew, I had been through everything I needed to today. Justin was off running errands for his boss, so I went in search of the car, gave up, and texted Felix. He told me where he was, and I located the car and got in, then asked him to take me to a grocery store so I could get something for dinner before he took me home. I don't know what I had thought, but I guess I figured that working in television was easy.

It sure as hell wasn't.

"ROSCO," I called as I came in the door lugging my groceries. He sauntered out, stretched, and then followed me into the kitchen. "I know. You're used to me being home to work, and now you're spending a lot of time alone." I picked him up, cradled him for a few minutes, then sat in one of the chairs. Rosco wiped his tail in my face a few times before settling down to purr.

A knock on the door startled me, and Rosco jumped down and headed over. I picked him up so he wouldn't make a run for it and pulled the door open, having no idea who could be visiting. Maybe a neighbor was welcoming me to the building?

"Meyer," I said, surprised enough that I nearly dropped Rosco. I stepped back, and Meyer came inside.

"You brought your cat," Meyer said. I set him down, and Rosco wound around Meyer's legs a few times, then stretched and sank

33

his claws into Meyer's thigh. "Jesus." He jumped back, and Rosco sauntered off toward the bedroom like he'd done his duty and wasn't needed anymore. "What was that for, you cantankerous cat?"

"I don't think he likes the fact that you took off." I wondered what Meyer could want. He certainly hadn't come here to be scratched by my cat, though I was going to have to give Rosco an extra treat for his appropriate welcome. "What can I do for you?" I asked, remembering my manners. I turned and went into the kitchen, pulled out a couple of microbrews, and brought them into the living room, holding out a bottle to Meyer.

"I see you still drink these," Meyer said as he turned the bottle in his hand before screwing off the top.

"You turned me on to them, and now the other stuff tastes like swill." I tipped the bottle and held it out. Eventually Meyer got the idea and clinked it with his. "What do you want?" I was tired and hungry, and I needed to fix some food and go to bed.

Meyer stood still, drinking his beer, and from the looks of it, trying to figure out for himself why he'd come. I sat on the sofa and leaned back. "What do you plan to say… about us?"

"I already told you. Nothing." I leaned forward with a sigh. "I think you're crazy, completely nuts, to be this afraid of something like the fact that you're gay and too ashamed of yourself and afraid to tell your family and the world the truth. None of your *adoring public* is going to care. Huge stars have come out of the closet. And your family…." I let that hang in the room.

"They would never speak to me again," Meyer said, draining the bottle in a couple of gulps. "I don't know why I came here. I guess I needed to know, and…."

"I am not going to tell anyone that you and I were lovers for three years. Three miserable, hiding, made-me-feel-like-a-complete-whore years." I met his gaze with steel. "I won't go back to that under any circumstances, so you get rid of whatever notion is running through the back of the fevered little brain of yours." I knew Meyer, and if he thought he could get a little boom-boom going, he would. Meyer ran hot, always did, and when he really got going, the world could come to an end and neither one of us would have stopped or given a damn. I'd missed that, if I was honest, but not enough to go back to the place I'd been in or how I'd felt about myself. "That's up to you to make the decision about when you're going to be truthful with yourself and the world."

"Dammit." Meyer flopped in the nearest chair. "You were always so damned fucking high and mighty. You knew what was best for me and for everyone else." Sarcasm dripped from his lips.

I shrugged. "Now that you have that understood, what did you come for?" I set down the bottle and crossed my arms over my chest.

"Why are you so antagonistic?" Meyer asked. "Things didn't work out with us—it's no big deal."

I tried not to let the jab hurt, but it did. Damn, I meant that little to him?

"We were together in one way or another for three years. I cared for you, saw you through a severe bout of flu and when you had that viral infection that nearly killed you. I was there all night long, sitting next to your bed, working a few hours, checking your temperature, and getting fluids in you. I put my damned life on hold for weeks until you were strong enough to get back to work, and I meant nothing to you?" I stood. "You know, if that's the case, then maybe you should leave. And while I promise I won't reveal any of your dirty little secrets, I'll be damned if I'm going to be nice to your slimy ass." I'd built up a good head of steam, and my mouth was really engaged.

"I didn't say that," Meyer interjected. "I meant that relationships end. It happens."

"That's true, but you slimed away rather than face the truth." Maybe it was good that I was getting all this out in the open. "You used me for years, and then when you got the chance, you were off to Hollywood."

"I asked you to come with me," Meyer said a little lamely.

I rolled my eyes. "As your dirty secret. You were never going to tell your family about me or live openly. Hell, you didn't in Philadelphia, and your family was thousands of miles away. Why could I expect anything different?" I looked down at my feet as Rosco returned and jumped into my lap. "I was in love with you, Meyer." Damn, that was hard to admit.

"I loved you too…."

The ache in his voice was unmistakable, and it tugged at my heart, but I pushed it away. I couldn't go back down that road again. I *wasn't* going to.

"I got out here and I didn't know anyone. There were so many times I nearly called you just to hear your voice and to have someone to tell me it was going to be okay." He sighed. "God, do you have another beer?"

I nodded and pointed to the kitchen. "Help yourself." This was not the kind of conversation I ever expected to be having with him.

He got up, and the refrigerator door opened and closed in the other room. Then he returned and flopped back down. "Everything wasn't easy for me either." He opened the bottle and sucked down a lot of the beer. "I had a lot of pressure on me from all sides."

I had heard that before. "Yeah, and if you had been honest and open, then I would have been there to help you through it all. Instead, you had all these secrets in all these little boxes that you were afraid would get out. You didn't want to tell your family that you were gay or about me, and for the longest time, you never told me you weren't out to your family or anyone else. You kept your work in some little box too, so when things weren't going well, you lied to me and said they were fine until you nearly lost your job and flushed your career down the toilet. You burned the candle at both ends, taking pills to work harder and longer instead of asking for help." I stroked Rosco's fur to try to calm myself even as my heart beat faster.

"I didn't want you to worry," Meyer explained. "You shouldn't have had to deal with my shit."

"But I was. I was in a relationship with you, even though I was still on the outside, looking in, excluded from so much of your world. So yeah, when you said you were leaving, it hurt, but I couldn't go with you because I was never really *with you* in the first place." That was the best way I could describe it. "I really need to get something to eat and then get to bed. This time change and the motion-sickness meds have really kicked my butt."

"Do you still like Asian? There's some wonderful Korean in the area, and they deliver." Before I could answer, Meyer had his phone out and was placing an order. "Two barbeque ribs with all the sides, no fish." Meyer gave the address. "I'll Apple Pay when you get here," he said, and then hung up. "That way you won't have to cook."

Sometimes I just didn't get him at all. "You don't need to do this."

It was hard for me to stay angry with him when he was actually nice, and that pissed me off. I *wanted* to be angry with him. That kept me from looking into his deep eyes and remembering just how his silken locks felt against my skin. Meyer was talented in the kitchen, but he had skills that were mind-blowing in another very important room of the house. I needed to push all that away, forget it like none of that existed. I couldn't allow myself to go there, or else I was going down a road that was only going to lead to more heartache. Meyer was not the kind of guy I could only be friends with. That would never, ever work. I was attracted to him the first time I saw him, I was in love with him when he left, and, damn it all, I could still feel his pull after all this time away.

I took a deep breath. We were going to have dinner, and then he was going home. Then we would work together on the show. Once it was over, he would stay, and I would leave, back to my life and to the real world. If I lasted that long.

CHAPTER 4

I SAT behind the desk with Rachel and Meyer on Friday of that same week as the chefs, mostly in white, filed onto the set. They looked around, craning their necks to see the various apparatus above and behind the area. The cameras were in position as well.

"All right. We will be taping all day today because we might use some of this footage during the show," Ethan said. "So let's look alive and be ready. Pay no attention to the cameras, and once we're done here, we will be filming with each of you to ask a number of questions and get some personal information that we can intersperse through the first episodes. We have a lot to get done today." He pointed to Rachel, who smiled.

"Chefs, welcome to *Cooking Masters*. You all are among the best of the best and were nominated to be on the show by your peers in a nationwide culinary talent search. We're pleased to have each and every one of you here with us. There will be many challenges ahead, more for some than others, but you are all worthy of being here." She turned to Meyer and then to me. "I want to introduce you to our judges. In addition to myself, I'm happy to introduce James Beard–award-winning chef and owner of multiple amazing restaurants on both coasts, Meyer Thibodeau."

Meyer stood as the contestants applauded.

"And we have food blogger and aficionado extraordinaire, Luke Walker, whose blog, *The Pickiest Eater in America*, is a sensation."

I smiled, and the contestants clapped and murmured among themselves.

"Please step forward, tell us your name, where you're from, and the kind of cuisine you love."

Each contestant stepped forward, introduced themselves, and explained why they loved to cook and the kind of food that fed their soul. There were men and women from every area of the country, cooking dishes from Jamaican jerk to traditional French, from nouvelle cuisine to reimagined classics. It was easy to see the enthusiasm in each and every face.

"Will we be cooking today?" one man from the back asked.

"Yes. This is not going to count and no one will be eliminated, but each of you should head into the kitchen behind you and prepare a signature dish using anything in the pantry. Again, this isn't going to send anyone home, and it isn't going to be on the show, but we will be judging, and the winner will receive dinner at Meyer's Ma Maison with Meyer, Luke, and myself. The winner will also get to choose another contestant to come along. You have an hour." Rachel smiled as they hurried into the other room, conversation breaking out as they rushed to find what they needed.

"Is it like this each season?" I asked in general. It seemed like chaos.

"Yes," Ethan answered before climbing onto his boom to oversee the shooting and direct the cameras. He had a computer, as well as a joystick, to control various cameras himself and to communicate with the others. It was like a dance, and I was fascinated by the process.

"We'll give them ten minutes to settle down and start working before we circulate through the room and see what they're doing. Feel free to ask questions and look at their work. It's often a good indicator of what we can expect, come judging."

We talked quietly and then slipped off our chairs and wandered in. Fourteen chefs were hard at work, chopping and sautéing. I peered into pans and smelled the beginnings of sauces.

"I read your blog all the time," one chef said before tossing some onions in a pan with butter and garlic.

"What are you making?"

"A pan-seared chicken thigh with a medley of vegetables," she answered.

I inhaled again. "It smells wonderful, but is that something you think is going to impress me and the others or just be something that I'll eat?" I met her gaze and could tell she was immediately rethinking her dish. Meyer wandered over, and I received a little smile. "This is a competition, for all of you," I said out loud. "I know I'm famous for being überpicky, but you're going to have to thread a needle with what you think I'm going to love and what Chef Meyer is going to enjoy as well." I really was beginning to see just how difficult this was going to be for them.

"I'm not sure that will work in the amount of time you have," Meyer was saying to a contestant, and I wandered over to him.

"Bacon," I said, inhaling. "Everything is better with bacon, but if you burn it, then nothing is worse." I smiled and moved away, Meyer coming along with me to stand back and watch them all work.

"I'm starting to see that the producers were brilliant," Meyer whispered, and instantly I saw a camera nearby. "I didn't get why they asked you on the show, but between the things you don't like and the standards I'm going to demand, along with intense flavors and subtle techniques, they are going to have to strike a real balance and get supercreative." And for the first time since I'd arrived in town, he actually smiled at me. Not a forced one or a TV smile, but a genuine one, and I remembered all those months when we were together and how that smile and a light touch could make things seem so much better than they were.

"Thirty minutes," Rachel called, and I pulled my attention back to the chefs. "Remember, your dishes need to be plated, and there must be three identical plates." I could see that she was a master at building tension, and I understood that while some drama was manufactured in editing, the clock itself created interest because it never slowed.

Our job at this point was to stand out of the way. I found my mind wandering, and I kept glancing at Meyer and then returning my attention to the chefs. Even though we were taping and there was a ton of activity around me, Meyer still pulled at me. I had to get my head in the game and pay attention. This was new and completely different for me, and I didn't want to screw it up.

"Five minutes," Rachel said.

The urgency ramped up. A dish dropped, pans clattered, a few chefs ran for plates, and I closed my eyes, expecting a collision that thankfully didn't come. I always wondered if stuff like this was built up by the show, the chaos growing as time ticked down and dishes were placed on the tables.

Rachel called time, and I stayed back a second, taking a breath, and then joined the others.

"What did you make for us?" I asked the first chef.

"Po' boy shrimp with a little sweet curry ginger sauce," she said.

Shrimp and I had a rocky relationship. I got sick on them once and found them difficult to eat, but I took a bite and forgot that experience with a touch of crispness, the heat of curry, and then the sweet finish.

"Very nice, good texture, sweet, heat, and a little crunch," I said with a smile, and we moved on to the next dish, which was a delight of salt, sweet, and citrus. I couldn't help closing my eyes as the chicken became a vehicle for a ton of flavor.

The next dish was a kind of soup, and I glanced at Meyer as he tasted it. Frankly, I was afraid of it. The color was off. I tasted it and made a face. "That tastes like day-old sweat socks."

The contestant winced as I put the spoon down.

We moved on to the next dishes until we had tasted them all. Then the three of us clustered to talk.

"Don't you think your comment was harsh?" Meyer asked.

"No. The soup tasted like feet and smelled worse." I glared at him. "How could you not taste it?"

"That was the radicchio," Meyer explained, rolling his eyes.

"So, a lettuce that smells like feet. What's next? Maybe mushrooms that smell like ass." I crossed my arms over my chest. "Meyer, I am going to give my opinion, and feet soup is pretty

41

awful." I knew everyone was watching, but I wasn't going to back down.

"Let's discuss the best dish," Rachel prompted.

"The shrimp and the chicken were amazing, both complex in flavor and texture. I could eat either one all day." I spoke to Rachel because Meyer was really getting under my skin and I hated that that was happening. The worst part was that he was being a pain in the ass, and yet heat raced through me like a fire tornado. How in the hell could this kind of disagreement get me hot? I was turning into a freak. The man might be a pain in the ass, but he was as stunning and confident as he acted, and that was attractive.

"I agree. The mushrooms were also outstanding," Meyer said, and Rachel nodded.

"What did you think of them?"

I thought a minute. "I hate mushrooms, and yet those weren't completely awful. There was some good flavor if I separated the dirt taste out of it. But I still think the shrimp was probably the best."

Meyer nodded, and Rachel did the same. We stepped out of the huddle and turned toward the chefs so Rachel could announce the top dishes.

"Meyer, will you announce the winner?"

He stood taller, and I could almost picture him as the dashing pirate in an old film, swinging from the rigging down to the deck, his hair fluttering in the wind, and his eyes bright, dashing and dangerous. "We all agree that the winner is Kelly and her shrimp." Meyer stepped forward, extending his hand. "Congratulations. You can choose another contestant to come to dinner with you."

She looked around and then picked the guy who had made the mushrooms, which was a good choice. If I was being honest, his dish probably deserved second place.

"Thank you all. I hope this was helpful to all of you in learning the kitchen and becoming familiar with how things will run. Don't expect them to become predictable, because there are plenty of surprises in store." Rachel smiled.

"Definitely. We have a lot to keep you on your toes," I added. "And as you saw, what you know about me, or think you know about me, isn't going to get you to the winner's circle." I was going to regret what I was about to say, but it needed to be said. "I'm not the only judge, and my likes and dislikes… well, they will be a part of this competition, but if you can surprise me and blow me away, that could take you far."

"Everyone, have a nice weekend," Ethan said. "We will begin contestant interviews today and continue them into early next week. Then the following week, we will be in here to film the season debut episode. This process is going to be grueling on us all, so get some rest while you can, practice, and hone your skills and ideas." Ethan stepped back.

"And remember that this is a competition. Alliances are one thing, but they aren't going to make you a better chef and won't make your dishes tastier. That only comes with hard work, attention to detail, and real skill."

I thanked them all, as did Meyer, and then they filed out surprisingly quietly.

"Do we get to see any of the stuff they talk about in the interview?" I asked Ethan.

"No. That part of the show is kept private until we air each episode," he explained, then rushed off to handle an issue as I caught up to Meyer.

"Dinner will be at seven on Sunday evening," Justin said as he hurried up to the three of us. "Cars will pick up Rachel and Luke. Meyer, you will be at the restaurant for part of the day, I'm sure."

"Yes. I'll get myself there." He was all business. "I'm working on a special menu for the dinner, and it's something I hope everyone will enjoy."

I wondered just what kind of menu he was thinking of. Knowing Meyer, it would be amazingly well done. But also knowing him, he could choose my favorite foods or decide to put together a menu featuring everything I hate in every course. Lord only knew.

"I'm looking forward to it," Rachel said. Her assistant approached and led her away, the two of them deep in conversation.

"Do you need anything?" Justin asked.

"Are we done for the day?" I wasn't sure if I was needed.

"Yes. We're done. The teams are working with the contestants, so both of you are free to go." Justin hurried after Ethan, and I sighed, deciding what I was going to do with the rest of the day.

"You did great," Meyer said. "Well, except for the feet thing. You described the food really well and seemed to enjoy most of it. You even equalized for the mushrooms in the dish to isolate what you hate."

"Are you trying to be condescending?" I told him. "First thing—I know food. I write about it nearly every day, and I'm going to speak my mind. That soup was disgusting and smelled like it had been reduced from someone's gym socks. I don't care that it was the radicchio that they used or anything else. If it tastes like feet, I'm going to say so." I shook my head as his lips got smaller. "Come on, even you have to admit there was something off with that soup."

Finally his lips twitched and he loosened up. "Yeah, okay."

"And it tasted like feet." I cocked an eyebrow. "Look, I'm going to be colorful. It's what I do on the blog and why they asked me here. You don't need to compete with that or feel threatened by it. Just go with it and continue to do your job."

"I just think it's unprofessional," Meyer retorted.

"And I'm not a professional," I countered. "I'm a guy who loves to eat." I sighed. "Do you remember all those Saturday mornings in Philly when you didn't have to go to the restaurant until the afternoon and you'd spend the day in my kitchen, working on new dishes and things you wanted to incorporate into your own restaurants? I learned what I know about food from you. You used to cook, and I'd eat, and everything was perfect." I pulled away because I could feel that warmth starting to build again. This was a bad idea, and I needed to keep a handle on what I was doing.

"I do." He motioned to the door, and I went along with him. "You hated some of the things I made, though."

"Yeah, because some were real clinkers." I laughed at a memory. "Remember the meat loaf you worked on for some concept of fancy home cooking? That stuff was so bad, even you admitted it and then took me out to dinner. The smell lingered in my kitchen for a week, and after we got back, Rosco refused to eat any of it. Those fails were rare, but when you did, you went big."

"Like the time the new fryer wasn't working and I nearly burned down my apartment." Meyer finally eased up a little.

"Yup. Or the soup that you added way too much onion to. It was good, but no one could come near us for a day and a half. Those were fun times, and we, both of us, were figuring things out. Though I will say you never made soup that smelled like feet."

"Okay." He put his hands up. "I know when I'm beaten."

We stepped outside, and Felix was waiting for me there. "I'll see you at the restaurant on Sunday evening. I can't wait to see what you have in store." I got inside, and the car started up. I didn't turn to watch as we pulled away, and Meyer stood watching the car in return. I didn't….

Okay, I lied.

ROSCO WASN'T happy that I was leaving and wouldn't stop brushing against me. I ended up getting dressed in the bathroom, feeding him, and then while he was busy, hurrying out.

Since Friday, it had been largely like being back home, with me working and him on my lap or lying at my feet. We kept each other company, and apparently he liked that. I did too. I wasn't needed on set until tomorrow, when I was to meet each of the contestants one-on-one for a few minutes. The team had apparently been shooting the interviews and the group out and about town. I continued the blog as usual, though naturally I wasn't allowed to say anything about what was happening on the show or that I was

45

even part of it. That was for the network to announce. But I wrote posts that I could shelve until I was able to post them and got a lot of client work accomplished, which was rewarding, if pretty lonely. The truth was, I was looking forward to dinner and some time out with people.

Felix was waiting for me downstairs and drove me to the restaurant.

"You should get dinner for yourself." I passed a fifty over the seat. "I'm going to be a while, and you deserve something good."

"I can't take that…," he protested, but I pressed it into his hand.

"Go have fun for a few hours, and I'll call when I'm ready." I thought he was going to refuse, but he took the cash with a smile. "We passed a few nice restaurants on the way. Have a good dinner."

He nodded. "Thank you. I'll get something to eat."

"Good." I opened the door and stepped out into the lighted night, heading into Ma Maison. The interior was classic Meyer: clean, with touches of warmth and just a sparkle of elegance. It really worked. The two contestants were at the bar having a drink, and I greeted them as I went through from the dining room to the kitchen.

"That smells wonderful," I told Meyer and turned, refusing to curl my lip up at the bananas stacked near the dessert station. After those years as Meyer's "friend," I knew my way around a kitchen, especially one of his. "Is everything going to be ready?" It seemed to be a one-man show tonight since he apparently had closed for this event.

"Yes. I'm serving everything family style. I wanted to showcase the food rather than the detailed presentation."

He could say what he wanted, but I knew the presentation would be as appealing as the food. It was part of what got Meyer to where he was.

"I think that will be nice. You are going to join us?" Steam went up from the stove, instantly sucked away by the hood.

"I'm going to need to prepare each course and…."

"Then tell me what you need." I was already moving to the sink to wash my hands. "Where is your help?"

"Sick with the flu. His kid had it and now he has it, and I gave the rest of the staff the day off. It isn't fair to pull them in when they have to work a full week coming up." Meyer continued working without stop, and I came around to him. "Keep an eye on that sauce and don't let it burn," Meyer said, "and sauté those mushrooms." He added ingredients to the pan, and I moved the mushrooms around the way he had shown me many times. "Perfect." He checked the oven, where a beef loin was roasting, the scent wafting upward to wrap around my senses and stoke my hunger. This was going to be one hell of a meal, I could tell.

The back door of the restaurant opened and banged closed. "You should have called, boss," a dark-haired bear of a man said in the deep voice of God. "Juan said he was sick, so I called Marie. She'll be right in." He peered over my shoulder.

"This is Luke. He's a friend from back home. Luke, this is the executive chef here at Ma Maison, Randall Usher."

"Is he on *Cooking Masters* too?"

"I'm an old friend of Meyer's." I would have shaken his hand, but Randall was already getting to work.

A woman, heavily tattooed and in her twenties, rushed in, heading to the dessert station. "We have this. Go be with your guests." She was already checking over her area.

I turned my duties over to Randall and left the kitchen, with Meyer a minute behind me.

"Thanks for diving in. I was getting a little in the weeds," Meyer told me as we exited the kitchen.

Rachel and Ethan were talking with the contest winners, and we joined them. "I can't wait to see what you have for us," she said as we approached.

The bartender had opened a bottle of sparkling wine, and he handed us each a glass. We toasted to a spectacularly successful season to come.

"And to an amazing dinner," I added, lifting my glass to Meyer. This—food and everything that went with it—was Meyer's passion. I swear, if he didn't have restaurants to work in and dishes to develop and make, he'd roll over and die. Being a chef was in his blood. It was who he was and how he identified himself.

"Hear, hear," the others echoed.

Meyer motioned to the chairs. I held out Rachel's seat, and she sat down. Then I took the chair next to hers. The bartender also acted as one of the servers, as did Randall and Marie. Meyer praised both of them in front of the group as plates were set on the table.

"A vegetable terrine, potatoes dauphinoise, and beef with chanterelles in a burgundy reduction, seasoned with garlic. Chicken in a light butter sauce with herbs and fennel. Great food doesn't need to be fussy, and it doesn't need to be so styled that you plate dishes with tweezers. Please enjoy." Meyer sat back the food was placed.

I was about to take a slice of beef when Marie took my plate and set down a new one with a gorgeous piece of beef, an amazing sauce, and not a mushroom in sight. "Thank you." I smiled up at her.

"Part of making good food and being a successful chef is knowing the people you're cooking for." Meyer gave me a wink, and I smiled right back, glad I had a napkin on my lap.

I took portions of the other dishes and slowly ate, relishing each bite. "This is heavenly, Meyer," I told him, and we shared a look that set my heart beating faster. Sometimes I wish I could control the damned thing, because it seemed to get excited at the things it shouldn't.

There was one thing I knew that the others in the room didn't. Meyer showed love with food, and his thoughtfulness at making me a version of the dish central to the meal without the mushrooms was, in a way, him saying that I was important. I took a deep breath to relax myself. I could easily be making more out of the gesture than Meyer intended. In fact, that was probably likely. I told myself that Meyer was just being a good host and returned my attention to the dinner.

"How did you do the chicken? It's so moist," Kelly asked, and Meyer went into his process.

The conversation centered around food—the meal specifically, but food in general—which wasn't a surprise at all. The food was amazing, and I tried not to overeat, but it was impossible.

"How long have you been doing the blog?" Rachel asked during a lull in the conversation.

"I started it three years ago." I didn't add the part about how, after Meyer left, I needed a way to channel my loss and exorcise what I thought was part of the reason he left me. "I've always been fussy, I know that, even as a kid, but my mom always said that us kids should try everything. The family used to make fun of me because everyone else ate just about everything. I was the 'picky' one."

"So they made you ashamed of it?" Kelly asked.

"Yeah. And I ate a lot of food that I could barely stand just because it was what was served." I leaned forward. "Let me ask you, is there something you don't like?"

"Yeah," Kelly admitted. "I'm originally from Maryland, but I don't like blue crabs. They taste muddy and weird. My dad didn't like them either, so Mom never bought them."

"Imagine if blue crabs were served as Tuesday night's dinner each and every week. That was how things were at home. Mom was determined that I would learn to like things, so she made them again and again. To this day, the smell of liver makes me leave the house. I cannot and will not eat it. No matter what, it will not go down. Things like mushrooms I used to eat by cutting them into small pieces and swallowing them whole so I didn't taste them. It was something that they were determined to break in me. They didn't. I just became ashamed of it and avoided foods I didn't like as soon as I had some freedom." I finished the beef and noticed that every eye at the table was centered on me. "Once I could drive, I would ask Mom for the car after dinner and go to the drive-through to get something to eat. I had food stashed under the bed in my room. Dry cereal, granola bars—stuff like that. I learned to cope, and I did that for a long time." I couldn't believe I was actually "coming out" like this. It was strange and yet freeing at the same time.

"Were there things you did learn to like?" Ethan asked.

"Yeah. I love coleslaw, though I never ate it as a kid. Most every vegetable when it's raw and in a good salad. As an example, spinach cooked is mushy and awful, but raw in a salad, it's amazing and one of nature's gifts. I love texture, and mouthfeel goes a long way. In my opinion, food should have body. Yet there are soft, smooth dishes that I adore. Risotto, when it's done right, is heavenly, but Meyer and I disagree on how it should be cooked. He likes it silky-smooth—I like it firmer." I met Meyer's scowl as he went into the proper consistency for risotto, and I smiled indulgently, rolling my eyes.

"That is the proper way," Rachel agreed.

"See, I don't agree. The proper way to make anything is the way the eater likes it," I said. "Food, a meal, it's a communication, a connection between the chef and the eater. At least that's how I look at it. That breaks down if one person doesn't enjoy it." I sat back, finished with the incredible meal. I knew there was dessert, but it was bananas. Meyer had decided to torture me at the end. "Do you all remember the four basic needs? Air, water, food, and elimination. For the longest time, I ate to live."

Everyone around the table blinked at me in astonishment.

"I don't get it," Kelly finally said.

"That same gorgeously done beef that Meyer made could have been slapped on a grill, cooked, cut into pieces, and consumed, and it would have given us the same caloric intake and energy as what Meyer served. It wouldn't be anywhere near as good, but it would have fueled our bodies. I ate like that." I stopped myself before I actually said out loud that Meyer had completely changed that for me. No one else here needed to know that.

"I don't think I could live that way," Kelly commented.

"I did in college," Rachel said. "Basic food that took away the hunger and let us stay up to study. There was no finesse, no real taste, just… food. I wouldn't want to go back to living like that."

"I doubt any of us would." I met Ethan's gaze. "That's part of why this show is important and does so well. It's entertaining, yes, but it also shows people that they can have more and do more than just make food to get them through." I raised my glass, and the others did as well. "To food as amazing as we've already had, and much more to come."

Randall and Marie cleared away the dishes, with the help of the bartender, and then dessert was served. Meyer did the honors, flaming the dessert at the table, making quite a show. Then Randall dished it up while Meyer pulled out another, smaller pan.

"We all know that Luke's hatred of bananas is legendary. So…." He flamed the pan, and the scent of cherries filled the restaurant. "I happen to know that he loves lots of other fruits, so for you, my version of cherries jubilee." He got it ready, topping a dish with a small amount of cake and homemade ice cream with the cherries. It was a feast for the eyes as well as the nose, and the taste burst on the tongue.

A digestif was served with dessert, and then shortly afterward, the party began to break up when Ethan said he had to go. Rachel said good night as well, and she left with the two contestants.

"That was amazing. And thank you for not feeding me bananas."

"You were right in what you said. A meal is a communication, and feeding someone something you know they aren't going to enjoy is a breakdown in communications." Meyer glanced around the empty room. "You and I sure had plenty of them." He pulled out a chair and sat back down. "I think they were all pleased."

"How could they be anything else? It was spectacular. That chicken was sublime, and the beef was perfection." I rested my hand on the table, and Meyer placed his on top. It was surprising and nice.

"Thanks, Luke. That means a lot."

Motion in the back room had Meyer pull his hand away and stand. I did the same, figuring it was time for me to go so they could clean up and get out of here themselves.

"Do you need help?"

"No. I have someone coming in first thing to take care of the dishes and reset the tables. You have a good night, and I'll see you for the first taping." The relaxed Meyer was gone in an instant, and I shook my head, messaging Felix that I was ready to be picked up.

"THIS WILL be our season debut episode," Ethan told the team in the first episode meeting. "We want it to be interesting and to set the tone for the rest of the season. Meyer, I need you to set a high standard for the food. Rachel, be as amazing as ever, and Luke, just have fun with it. Our guest judge is Chef Hank West. He's flying in from Las Vegas and is currently caught in traffic, but he will be here soon. The contestants are not to know that he is here until we announce it in the challenge. The packet in front of you describes the challenges that we will be using for this episode, and the details. It also contains the twist that we will be introducing. Treat that information as confidential. Do not talk about it with anyone."

I nodded along with the others as I reviewed the details. Rachel and I would be judging the first round with Chef Hank. It looked like I was going to be dropped into the fire, as it were.

"Are you up for what we have planned, Luke?" Ethan asked, and I continued down the page.

"Bananas," I said under my breath. "Really? You're jumping right in." I suppose it was best to get it over with. They had said they were going to use some of the things I hated.

"Yes, but if you look, you'll see it's an entrée challenge. So the dish is to be savory and feature bananas," Meyer explained. "You might like them that way." He was trying not to laugh, the bastard.

"Can you do it?" Ethan asked.

"Yes," I answered firmly. "I can do anything." I forced a smile and sat back, refusing to let them see how completely *un*thrilled I was.

"That's the spirit. And be as honest as you can." Ethan was clearly hoping for some sort of uncomfortable gold out of this. "Are there any other questions? If not, we will begin shooting tomorrow morning. Meyer, when Hank arrives, you and I will walk him through what he needs to do. If there's nothing else, we all have work to do." He was up and on his way out of the room before anyone could move, with the camera people and other technicians right behind him.

"Wow, what got into him?" I asked Rachel, hoping she might know.

"The network had an unexpected cancellation that left a hole in the schedule, and they want to air the shows two weeks earlier. They're starting the promo in a week, but we have nothing for them to use to promo."

I sighed. Out of the frying pan and into the fire for all of them. "Did they move up the shooting schedule?" That would explain the pressure in Ethan's voice and demeanor.

She nodded. "The first episode will be shot on the current schedule, but the second and third will follow right behind without a break. Normally we shoot, digest, learn, plan, and then shoot the next, but we're going to have to plan the next episodes while we shoot the current one. It happens." She shrugged and then checked her phone. "I better get things ready, and I think you should too."

I waited for Meyer and relayed what I had just been told. It seemed he already knew and was taking it in stride.

"Don't worry. You're going to be great at this."

"I hope so." The added pressure was increasing the doubt in the back of my mind. I needed to keep it in check. I could be good at this if I didn't sabotage myself.

"You will. I know it."

The warmth in Meyer's eyes told me that he meant it. Damn, I'd thought I was over the man, but just that look, full of care and concern, was enough to make my heart stir. And what was worse, I thought I saw my feelings reflected back at me.

"If you feel you need some help, let me know and I'll be glad to work with you."

"Thanks. We'll have to see how this first episode goes." I inhaled deeply to try to calm my nerves. "I was going to head over to wardrobe to make sure everything is planned out." I had to do something, otherwise I'd just worry.

"Do that and call me tonight if you want to talk anything through." Meyer excused himself when Justin signaled him, and I headed out to try to make sure I was as prepared as I could be.

CHAPTER 5

I'D FED Rosco and was caught up on other tasks, so I sat at my makeshift desk trying to figure out what I wanted to do. Sitting inside all evening didn't seem appealing, and there was nothing on television that I wanted to watch. "What do we want to do?" I asked the cat, bored out of my mind.

A soft knock on the door saved me from answering my own question at the moment. "Meyer," I said with a smile when I found him standing outside. He seemed to turn up when I least expected it.

"Come on," Meyer said. "Go get a jacket and let's go."

I shook my head, closing the door after he stepped inside. "Huh."

"You're sitting around in here fidgeting and vacillating. There's an entire city out there that's filled with amazing things to do and see." He shrugged. "You lived in Philadelphia all your life and never saw the inside of Independence Hall." Meyer sighed.

I turned and got a light jacket, then returned to where Meyer waited, grateful to have something to do. "You don't need to do this. I'll be fine. I figured out how to do things on my own."

Meyer didn't roll his eyes or say anything. He simply stared at me, hard, and I felt myself withering a little under the intensity of that gaze. No wonder he was a television star. He smoldered, and with a single look, he could convey so much intensity.

"What?" I finally asked.

"You sit home behind that computer and bury yourself in it." His gaze didn't move, and I quivered slightly as he licked his lower lip. "Come on. I'm taking you out." He stood near the door and again stared, challenging me to argue. I sighed softly because this was a bad idea. "I've known you for a long time. You and I can be friends and do things together."

"I see." I followed him out and locked the door. "You and I are going to be friends. Is that it?"

Again with the damn smile that went all the way to his eyes. "Why not?" Meyer said it so casually, I wanted to slap him and tell him exactly why this was a bad idea.

Because you shattered my heart and made me feel bad about myself when we were together. Because… because…. His eyes were so deep and gorgeous, and my arguments slipped from my mind.

I took a step back. "Because I'm not sure it's a good idea."

My answer didn't seem to faze him. "Come on. Let's go have some fun. And I know just the place." He turned and walked down the hall to the elevator. I followed him, against my better judgment, because… what the hell?

We got in, rode down to the ground floor, and went out through the lobby to Meyer's BMW. I got in, and he drove to the freeway. Soon we were whizzing through the city, lights and cars passing at high speed until Meyer veered off and we were in a quieter, darker area.

"There are woods in LA?" I asked as we passed slowly down a tree-lined road.

"This is Griffith Park, and it's right in the middle of the city."

We passed through a tunnel, then turned left, climbing upward, and went in circles until we reached a bluff that burst with light and activity.

"What is this?"

"Griffith Observatory. I thought the geek in you would love it. The building has been expanded, but the main portion is Depression era, done under the Works Progress Administration. There are telescopes, a planetarium, and space and science displays." He parked, and we walked across the great lawn in front of the building. It was stunning, with people playing on the grass, and yet it was largely quiet.

I figured we'd go inside, but Meyer led me toward the side, and we climbed the stairs to the roof and then walked along to the back and the edge of the escarpment. The entire city with its grid of lights was laid out as far as the eye could see. It danced and twinkled in the night air.

"I like to come up here when I need a chance to get away and take a breather. Down there is everything you could possibly imagine: wealth, money, power, the industry that entertains half the world. The Pacific is in that direction." Then he pointed behind me, and I turned. "The Hollywood sign, which was originally built for a housing development."

"Wow." A breeze came up, and I pulled my jacket around me. Not that I was cold, but maybe a little exposed or overwhelmed. How did anyone learn anything in a city this size? It was fascinating and frightening at the same time. Well, at least I wasn't staying here all that long.

"I love that view. It's like all the potential and promise of everything you could ever want laid out right in front of you. All that's required is the desire and drive to go get it." Meyer leaned on the railing as he looked.

"It's just lights and a lot of people." Up here was quiet; down there was a battle with chaos fighting for order. And most of the time, it seemed to me that chaos was winning. "Can we go inside?"

Meyer checked the time. "Yes. I got us tickets for the show. It starts in fifteen minutes, so you and I should head inside to get a good seat. Afterward, you can look around."

I retraced our steps down and then entered the atrium, painted in that distinctive, blockily beautiful WPA-style. We passed around a huge pendulum, and I peered down one story to where it nearly reached the floor and then up to the decorated dome where it originated.

"Come on. We should take our seats." He led the way to the back and into the planetarium theater, directing us to seats just before the doors closed and night descended around us.

The seats reclined, and stars came out on the dome. The narration began, and we took an awe-inspiring trip through the night sky. Constellations, galaxies, planets—all of them passed by, paying us a visit as we took an amazing journey. In the darkness, Meyer sat next to me, and as we passed Saturn with its rings, he took my hand. Together he and I hurtled through space. Stars exploded and created new elements and dust clouds that condensed into new planets right before our eyes. It was amazing, and I squeezed Meyer's hand as we took the journey together, the way I had once thought that I would travel through life with him. That he and I would build our own world and make our own way. It had been a nice fantasy then, and I let it wash over me now.

Then we returned to LA and the sunrise, the rebirth of our own star that we witnessed each morning. Meyer's hand slipped out of mine as the lights came up. The trip through the universe was over, and it was time to return to the real world.

"Thank you for coming, and we hope you enjoyed your tour of the universe."

Everyone clapped and then stood to head for the exits. I waited for my turn and filed out with Meyer. The trip had been fun. "Thanks." I kept wondering what Meyer wanted from me… or thought he wanted.

We toured the rest of the exhibits, watched a demonstration of the Tesla coil and its artificial lightning, enjoyed the remaining exhibits, and then headed out. Meyer and I wandered the grounds and then went back to the car.

"Where to next?"

Meyer smiled. "How about something to eat? BCD Tofu." He unlocked the car door and, once inside, we were off again. The Korean diner was packed, but Meyer got a table and ordered for me, knowing what I liked. The dumplings were heavenly, the sweet spicy ribs a treat, and we laughed together. Maybe that was the best part.

"So there I was, completely lost. I'd been here just a week and was supposed to be having dinner with some backers at this new, hip, fancy restaurant downtown, but the GPS in the car was all messed up. It kept sending me all over the place, changing directions. It was a mess. Somehow I ended up here, and I phoned to tell them where I was and that I was lost."

"Oh God."

"Nope, one of the backers loves this place, and he brought them all over and we ate here, closed the deal, and that was the beginning of Ma Maison. Now BCD is a good-luck place for me. I come here to celebrate."

I nodded. "What are we celebrating tonight?"

The smile slipped from Meyer's lips. I had to open my big mouth and ruin it. I could never just keep quiet and accept things for what they were. I should know better.

"I…." He nodded. "You know, we are celebrating. Somehow the world conspired to bring you back in my life, and that is worth a celebration. I need to learn to be grateful for the good things that happen, rather than worrying about what might happen."

The server brought the bill, and Meyer pulled out his wallet to hand her the money for the check. Then we were off again, buzzing back down the freeway. I liked traveling at night. During the day, the freeways were majorly congested, but at night it was a different story. Traffic was lighter, and it moved, the city passing outside. We took the now-familiar exit and pulled up to the building where I was staying. By some miracle, there was parking right in front, and I let us into the building and the apartment. As soon as I closed the door, Meyer stepped close, cradled my cheeks in his heated hands, and kissed me.

It took me by surprise, but my lips and body remembered just what Meyer did to me, and that touch was so familiar, yet new and hot. This was wrong, but I didn't care in the least. I had missed him, my body and mind—hell, my spirit—had missed how Meyer could make me feel, and I needed it. I threw caution to the wind and let him guide me through the living room. I completely ignored the fact that we nearly tripped over the coffee table.

Meyer chuckled even as his hand slipped under my shirt and tweaked my nipples. I gasped and pressed forward, wanting more. "Damn, you're so responsive. How long has it been?"

I ignored the question and pulled Meyer toward the bedroom.

"Luke?" he pressed, but I kept going. I wanted to make him not remember that he even asked, kissing him, winding my arms around his neck. I had wiles too, and one of them was the ability to make Meyer forget his goddamned name. If kissing were in the Olympics, I'd win the gold medal, no doubt about it. I could make a guy forget his name, and anything else, just by kissing him the exact right way.

We reached the bed, and I heard Rosco jump down, probably hurrying out of the room, not that I watched him at that very moment. I was way too busy with Meyer pushing me down onto the mattress.

"Damn, you don't smell the way you used to, better now," Meyer whispered. "Though you do act like you did." He paused, backing away. "No one ever did what you do to me." He heaved for breath, and I smiled, knowing I could still do that to him.

"Have there been a lot of people since you left?" I sat up, wrapping my arms around Meyer's waist and running them up under his shirt, pulling it along with my hand, baring his skin so I could nuzzle him, get a taste of him again. I knew this was a terrible idea, but I wanted to know Meyer and to feel Meyer's excitement, even if it was only once.

"A few, but none in a while," Meyer answered shakily.

"Why?" I pursued, moving my hands up his back, taking the shirt up higher before slipping it over his head. I tossed the fabric to the floor, then ran my fingers over the sculpted muscles that rippled under his sun-kissed skin.

Meyer hesitated, and at first I didn't think he would answer. "None of them was you."

I stopped and pulled away so I could look into his eyes. "Then why didn't you call?" I was shocked.

"Because I didn't think I had the right. I was the one who left, and things weren't exactly perfect between us. You were going on with your life, and I should have been getting on with mine. And I did, in every way but… well… you know."

"I see. You were always afraid that if you got close to someone, they might find out who you were. The walls of your closet are still as strong as they have always been." I didn't want to talk about this any longer. I had Meyer in my bedroom, half naked, and taking a walk down memory lane wasn't high on my list of priorities.

"What about you?" Meyer pressed.

"Let's just say that you're hard to replace." I flashed a smile, and Meyer clutched me to him, the kiss intense enough that my attention returned to where it was supposed to be. The excitement that had waned between us grew once again, deepening and wiping away the shadows of the past, at least for now.

I pulled Meyer down, kissing him with everything I had. His weight was solid and firm, surrounding me in heat. I wanted more and squirmed slightly in order to get my shirt off, sighing at the skin-to-skin contact. I held Meyer as tightly as I dared. He shook in my arms, and I groaned against his lips, letting him know that I was just as into this as he was.

Meyer broke the kiss when it seemed I was seconds from passing out. If I could have suspended my need for breath, I would have just so I could continue kissing him without a break.

"Get your clothes off," I whispered.

Meyer rolled alongside me. Then his shoes and socks dropped to the floor, followed by the rest of what he was wearing. I shucked my own clothes, watching him. Damn, Meyer was just as fine as he'd always been. Strong, lean, built wide and sturdy, pushing all of my buttons. Physically, Meyer had been it for me. He was my ideal, and I hated to admit it, but the model I compared every other guy to.

"Come here." I beckoned, and Meyer drew closer, stalking me until he climbed back onto the bed. I pulled him on top, wrapping my legs around his waist.

Being with Meyer was like exploring a path walked some time ago and then forgotten, now rediscovered, only to be experienced once again. Joy remembered and joy experienced, both at the same time. That was what I wanted and received.

"What could I have been thinking?" Meyer whispered as our gazes met, his filled with heat and passion, his eyes wet, shining down at me.

"I don't know," I whispered back. "Sometimes we do things because we think they're best for us, I guess. Most of the time we're wrong."

Meyer laughed, his gaze not moving an inch. "That is so very pessimistic."

"No. It's true. We fumble in the dark so many times, thinking we understand the consequences of our decisions, and then we're surprised when we're disappointed with the results." I paused. "Just for the record, I was never disappointed with you. Maybe in some of your decisions, but never with you."

Meyer kissed me, driving me higher as his fingers worked their magic. I squirmed and shivered under their light ministrations, each touch like adding kindling to a fire, and as he continued, the flames built and built until there was no stopping the conflagration. I wanted the flames—in fact, I'd lost track of the number of times I'd prayed for them. Here Meyer was, offering them again, and I took them. I held on with both hands as he used his tongue to delight me, worrying the secret spots that it seemed only he had ever taken the time to find. My head spun, and I closed my eyes—not because I didn't want to see him, but because I could only take so much amazingness at once. My senses threatened to overload, and I struggled to keep them in check as Meyer slowly entered me, filling me in a way I hadn't been in so long, touching me deeply enough that I worried my soul was never going to be the same. And yet I managed to hold on to it and keep it intact. I had to, because I had to keep my heart and soul in one piece. It was the only way I was going to survive.

"Faster," I begged into his mouth, my words swallowed by his breath. I was on the cusp, holding back but tiring, and as Meyer drove me higher, I gave up control of my body and pleasure to him, and instantly I sailed in the wind, soaring to incredible breathless heights, where Meyer held me until I slowly came back down to earth.

I closed my eyes as our bodies separated, covered in sweat and happy, sated, and content. I had no idea how long Meyer planned to stay, and I didn't want to rock the boat. Thankfully, I was able to close my eyes and doze for a few minutes. Meyer ran his hands over my chest, holding me, and for a minute, I could believe that things were the way they had been… almost.

CHAPTER 6

THE TAPING of the first episode was well underway. The appetizer round had gone off without a hitch, and I actually had a good time. Rachel, Hank, and I all agreed on the winning dish, and Magnus, the winner, had been thrilled with his five-thousand-dollar prize.

"The main course round is where the rubber hits the road," Meyer was saying, and I had to keep my focus on the here and now as I stood in the kitchen with the other judges.

"Yes." Rachel took over seamlessly. "This is one of our Luke Walker challenges. We figured we'd start with a good one and see what you all could do. You are going to have to walk a fine line with this one. As most of you know, Luke's hatred of bananas is legendary. You all need to make a savory dish that features bananas, and you will be serving it to the four of us, as well as a group of ten Central Valley fruit farmers who are in town for a water conservation symposium. You will have just ninety minutes to prep, cook, and serve in the *Cooking Masters* dining room. And remember, at least one of you will be going home." She looked at each of us and then back at the group. "Your time starts... now."

Pandemonium broke out as the fourteen chefs raced to the pantry to get their ingredients. The cameras panned away from us, and we left the set. I headed out for a chance to rest a little. I had no idea how stressful it would be to be in front of the camera like that.

"You did really well," Rachel said from behind me, and I turned to her as I reached my trailer. "Don't worry about the cameras and where they're located. It isn't our job to get the shot— it's theirs. Honestly. This isn't a movie where we're trying to get something specific."

I sighed and opened the door. "Thanks. I'm sure I'll get the feel for it by the time we wrap up the season." I smiled, and she chuckled.

"Honestly, you'll be fine." She continued to the next trailer and went inside.

I went inside, got a water, and sat on the sofa, closing my eyes to let some of the tension ease. And it was working until my phone rang.

"Hi, Clare," I said after glancing at the display.

"How is it going?" she asked.

"It's fine. How are you there?" I wasn't even going to talk about the show. It was best to avoid the subject in case I spilled the beans on something. "Is everything going okay?"

"Yes. I miss you and Rosco, though. I picked up your mail, and I'm sending the nonjunk in a box to your address in La La Land. It doesn't seem like there's anything urgent, but you can pay your bills and crap." She seemed as energetic as ever. "You sound stressed."

"Doing one of these is harder than I expected. But I'm okay. Just resting before I have to go back." I said goodbye, hung up, and probably should have grabbed my computer to work, but that wasn't going to happen. Meyer thrived in front of the camera—he got energy from it—but it drained me of all that I had.

A soft knock sounded and then the door opened. "They're going to need you in five minutes to see what the chefs are doing." The door closed again, and I heaved myself up off the sofa to head to the set.

It was still a hive of activity, and I joined Meyer as he made his rounds. It was hard not to stop and just watch him. "What do you think? Anything so far that might change my mind about bananas?"

"Try this," Meyer offered, and I tasted from the pot, shivering. "I take it not."

"I thought cooked bananas might be different, but that's… just banana-y." I did my best to chuckle and suppress the urge to wipe my mouth out.

"It will taste different once I'm done, I promise," Jean Claude said in a French accent as he continued working.

Meyer and I talked with a few more chefs before stepping away to let them cook. "We are going to need to change clothes for the judging," Meyer told me, and we left for wardrobe.

"How am I going to do this?" I asked him. "That room smelled awful, and I don't want to taste anything."

Meyer paused as soon as we were outside. "Pretend it's something else and don't fixate on the banana. There are going to be spices, beef, chicken, and a number of other things into the mix. Concentrate on those as best you can." He patted my shoulder, and as I headed for the wardrobe area, I could still feel it… and for the millionth time, I wondered about how things would be after Meyer's visit last night.

I had half expected him to be cold and distant, but he wasn't. Meyer acted pretty much the same, except maybe a little nicer, and some of his impatience had definitely vanished. There hadn't been any outward affection, not that I'd expected any. Still, I was going to keep a certain amount of distance. I needed that in order to ensure that I didn't fall back into what happened with him before. This time things were going to be different. They had to be.

Wardrobe had my clothes ready, and I carried them back to my trailer to change. Once dressed, I stopped in at makeup for a check that everything was still in place, then headed to the set.

Time was running down, and we went into the dining area, where the other guests were gathering. There was an air of excitement in the room, and we all took our places as time ran out for the chefs and the cameras were activated.

"Thank you all for coming, and I hope you enjoy the meal," Rachel said once everyone had sat.

The chefs brought in their dishes three at a time, explaining each one. The first round was placed before me, and I stared at my food nemesis. I had hoped that they might try to disguise the bananas as other food, but each dish smelled like, well, bananas. I tried to follow Meyer's advice and tasted each component, concentrating on the nonbanana items.

"What do you think?" Meyer asked.

"Well…." I could feel everyone turn to me. "The beef is perfectly cooked, but the banana seems weird to me. Like it really doesn't belong. The sweet is fighting with the rest of the dish." I kept quiet about the fact that I wanted to spit out part of it. "The vegetables with banana is actually nice. The spice works, and it lets the banana be the sweet note while enhancing the flavor of each component." I took a bite of the fish, nearly choked but swallowed it, then pushed the rest of the food around on my plate.

"What do you think of the fish?" one of the guests asked.

"I wouldn't feed this to my cat, and if I did, Rosco wouldn't have anything to do with it."

The others tittered but agreed it wasn't good at all. Meyer nearly did a spit take.

"You have a cat?" Hank asked as the dishes were removed and next set of chefs brought in their food. "Is he as picky as you?"

"Worse, if that's possible," I answered.

"It's true," Meyer added. "I've seen Luke mix fancy canned food and dry because his cat likes a variety of textures. He won't eat either food alone. It has to be both, and only certain kinds."

Meyer turned to the chefs as their dishes were presented, and once they'd left, their dishes were tasted and discussed. I had to admit that they weren't bad.

"Have you and Meyer known each other long?" The conversation flowed between courses just like at a dinner party.

Even though I was asked the question, I hesitated.

"Luke and I were friends in Philadelphia before I moved here. We've known each other for a number of years, but lost touch after

I left. I don't think it was something that either of us intended to happen. It just did." That sounded honest and was probably as close to the actual truth as Meyer was ever going to admit to anyone.

"Yeah, and I started the blog and then was asked to be on the show. I didn't know Meyer was going to be a judge too." I could play the old-friend game if that was what Meyer wanted, but I was surprised at how it hurt.

"What would your cat think of this round?" one of the farmers asked, and the conversation returned to Rosco. The camera operators seemed enthralled and narrowed in.

"I think he'd be well fed," I answered. "And I'd be worried about him getting overweight. Rosco is a greedy eater, so I have to watch him like a hawk." Talking about Rosco gave me something to occupy my mind for a few seconds.

The conversation continued around the table and shifted back to food as the rest of the dishes were served. I only took a few bites and didn't try to eat all of anything. I needed to ensure I didn't get full and could keep each of the dishes straight.

"Thank you for joining us for the evening," Rachel said as the chefs all came out, and the group applauded. "And thank you, chefs, for the food." Everyone at the table lifted their glasses in salute, and the chefs filed back out again. The diners broke up after that, and we four judges saw everyone out.

I wasn't sure if we would film the judging right away, but Justin motioned toward that part of the set, so I followed the others inside and took my place. Rachel controlled the discussion, which was orderly. We discussed each dish and reached a decision on the winner and the loser. We were told not to censor what we thought. They would edit it for maximum impact and so the outcome wasn't too much of a giveaway. Personally, I thought "food I wouldn't feed to my cat" was probably a pretty good clue, but we reached our decision, called in the chefs, and rendered our verdict, with the man who made the "not cat food" being sent home.

"That's a wrap," Ethan said once they had all they needed. "Very good show, everyone. Tomorrow we'll set up, and then we'll tape the next episode. Luke, if you have a minute."

I nodded and followed Ethan off to the side.

"How well did you and Meyer know each other?" Ethan asked.

"As he said, we were friends. I didn't know he was going to be on the show until he showed up. It's been three years since we've last seen each other." I repeated the line.

"There are people watching everyone all the time. Secrets have a way of getting out for all of us."

I met his gaze, but my insides were turning to mush. I wasn't ashamed of who I was, but I had promised Meyer that I would keep his secret, and I meant it.

"I'm a blogger from Philadelphia. Why would anyone care about me and my past? I've never been on anyone's radar, and as soon as the show is over, I'll disappear and no one is going to care about me once again."

"Are you kidding? Your reactions during dinner were gold. Each dish was written all over your face, and it was priceless. Don't you dare change. If you thought the dish was bad, you had an expression that every single person out there could identify with. They are going to make memes of that, and you'll probably get your own emojis." Ethan was practically giddy. "But that also means that the press and the public are going to want to know everything about you."

"Well, that's just thrilling."

Ethan half smiled. "It's what comes with this business. Most people are going to be nice and pretty respectful. But there will be the rabid ones, and they'll dig into your private life for anything juicy." He glanced to where Meyer and Rachel stood talking. "Meyer has been in that spotlight for years now, and they love him."

ANDREW GREY

"Okay…?" I prompted. Ethan had to have checked me out before he and the producers agreed to have me on the show. They had to know that I was gay. This was the Cooking Channel, though. They had gay people on their shows all the time.

"I see the way you look at Meyer and the way he looks back. If there isn't something going on between you… then you both need to make sure nothing happens. This is a respected show, and the number one on this network. We want good food, great television, and no scandal. That might get short-term ratings, but it's long-term death and everyone knows it."

"I see." There was no way in hell I was going to confirm or deny anything. Even breathing an answer would in some way break my promise to Meyer. "Well, it's a good thing that I'm not interested in fame, at least not the Hollywood kind. I'm here to be a judge on your show and then go home. That hardly seems the kind of situation that is going to be conducive to me getting in trouble with anyone." This entire conversation was so much like the one I'd had with my parents when I came out of the closet. Plenty of euphemisms and vague references because it made them more comfortable than actually just saying the words. Sometimes we all need to just drop the drag and say things the way they were. "Is there anything else that you need?"

"No. You did great. Keep it up." He flashed a smile as his phone rang. He snatched it up and wandered away as he talked.

I rolled my eyes and shook my head. I probably should have expected something like that eventually.

I messaged Felix and asked him to meet me near the soundstage door in fifteen minutes. He responded right away, and I joined Rachel and Meyer. "I'm going to go unless either of you need anything."

"It was a great show, and the next one is going to be better," Meyer said.

Rachel turned to me. "That cat comment was genius. Half the country is going to be wondering all about the picky eater guy with

70

an equally picky cat." She grinned and rubbed her hands together for a second. "I need to go and get some beauty sleep. I'll see you boys in the morning." She bounced off, and I turned to Meyer.

"What's with her?"

"She met someone." Meyer winked. "Rachel has the worst luck in men, but started seeing a man a few weeks ago at a restaurant downtown."

I snickered. "You set her up, didn't you?" Meyer was a matchmaker—he couldn't really help it. His mother was one too, and so were most of the women in his family. It was part of what made them special. The tradition had come over from the old country, and his family had kept it alive.

"All I did was invite her to a friend's restaurant so she could check out his food and see if he'd make a good guest judge for the show." Meyer bumped my shoulder. "It was a no on the show, but it seems a big, fat, glowing yes from Rachel." There were times when he could stoke the drama. I loved that about Meyer. He leaned closer. "She's a major size queen, and Lord knows he has exactly what she wants." Meyer snickered, and I covered my mouth, grateful there was no one around.

"I need to go. I'll see you tomorrow." I turned to leave and realized that Meyer was following me.

"Do you want me to come over later?" Meyer asked, and I nearly said yes right away, but took a deep breath. That was exactly how things had been in Philadelphia. That exact same road was opening up in front of me.

"If you like, but you and I need to talk." I turned, meeting his heated gaze with cold steel. "I mean, really talk. So yeah, come on over. I'll have a beer waiting for you." I left without further explanation and headed to where Felix was waiting in the car. I climbed in and shut the door, letting Felix drive me home while my heart and head fought with each other. This wasn't a battle or a skirmish, but a full-out war—the Russian Front, Maginot Line kind of war. And I needed to figure out which side I was truly going to land on.

The shitty part was that I honestly had no fucking idea.

"COME ON in," I told Meyer an hour later. I handed him a beer and motioned toward the sofa. I sat in the nearest chair, with Rosco settling on my lap. At least I knew I'd have him on my side, no matter what. "I can't do this again," I informed him. "I won't go back to the way things were three years ago. I won't be your little secret on the side. I'm out and I have a life."

"With your cat?" Meyer sniped.

"Don't be a shit. You don't get to judge me. I know who I am, and sneaking around, having a half life with someone that only exists behind closed doors and on the sly, isn't it. That doesn't mean that I don't care for you. I always have, but I can't live that way. I did it for three years, and it damned near killed me." I tipped my beer to my lips and took a drink. "That isn't who I can be, and it isn't fair. I spent a great deal of time and pain figuring out who I was, and those years in Philly made me ashamed of myself. I had to hide and stay out of the light because of you. I can't do that again."

"But I…." Meyer drank his entire beer and set the bottle on the table. "My family…."

"I can't live a lie, and you've been doing it for so long that you don't know anything else. Living a lie takes so much effort." I set my bottle on the table near his. "I know that Hollywood is like living in a fishbowl, but the network isn't going to care if you're gay or not, and neither are your customers at the restaurants. This is LA, where half the people are gay and the other half don't give a damn." I leaned forward.

"You want me to come out. Is that the price of being able to see you? Is that what you're saying?" I could tell that Meyer was becoming agitated.

"I want you to be honest with yourself and the world. I know you're afraid of your family. But what can they do to you? You're hugely successful, on television—a chef who is looked up to and respected. Being gay has nothing to do with the amazing food you make, or your ability to run your businesses. Do you really think your family will turn their backs on you?" I had a pretty good idea that they might disapprove, but I also knew that Meyer helped them out. "I really doubt it."

"You don't know what it's like. I could come out and they could support me. But what about their friends? The community? They'll be whispered about behind their backs and…." Meyer stood. "I think I'd better go."

I nodded. "Yeah. I think you should. I know we aren't going to agree on this one." I followed him to the door, my hand on the knob, but I didn't pull it open. Instead, blocking his way, I let go and gently caressed his cheek. Meyer closed his eyes, and I could almost feel the conflict raging inside him. I knew what it felt like and how hard this was for him. "I will say this. Regardless of what you think will happen, what we fear is almost always worse than reality." I patted his shoulders. "These are very strong, but they're carrying a burden you don't need to haul. I promise I'll be here if you want to talk, but think about what you want and how you truly want to be." I let my hands slide away from his shoulders and opened the door.

I refused to watch him step out the door. I really wished things had been different.

CHAPTER 7

THE NEXT week was the busiest of my life, and that included when I worked full-time, was just starting the blog, and was trying to get my own business off the ground. I managed to write in my dressing room during down times in order to keep up with the blog and my clients' work. Most of the time when I wasn't on set, I was preparing to be on set. I even began bringing Rosco with me to the trailer because he soothed my nerves, which were becoming raw and more jangled by the day.

"Don't let Rosco out," I called when the door opened.

"I won't," Meyer said.

I sat up. He and I hadn't talked very much, other than for work, in the week since he'd come to the apartment.

Meyer closed the door and brought Rosco over, handing him to me without getting scratched. Rosco seemed to have mellowed in his opinion of Meyer. "They are going to be ready to begin taping the appetizer in half an hour. There was a problem with one of the stoves, and they want to get it fixed first."

Meyer sat on the edge of the sofa, with Rosco curled between us, and absently stroked down his back. "I talked to my family. Mom and Dad skyped with me last Friday night, and I was tired and they were nagging me about getting married, so… I told them." He closed his eyes and began shaking. Rosco got up and stretched onto Meyer's lap, lying across his legs. Rosco always knew when I needed his comfort, and I guess he thought Meyer did now.

"How did they take it?" I asked, but pretty much had my answer from Meyer's posture.

"Well, they didn't open their arms and start singing 'Kumbaya,' if that's what you're thinking. My mother cried, and my father yelled.

74

Then, when I couldn't take it any longer, I told them goodbye and that I'd call them again when they'd had a chance to think things over." He sighed. "My father sent me a message yesterday telling me that they didn't need to talk to me unless I decided to lead a Christian life. I've been helping them every month, and Dad said that he and Mom don't need any of my tainted money anymore." He lifted his gaze. "They would rather go without than accept me."

I shook my head. "I'm sorry." I wish I could have seen that coming, but I had never met his parents. The one time they'd come to Philadelphia, I wasn't introduced. "Do you think they'll come around at all?"

Meyer shrugged. "Mom might, but my dad won't, ever. This has become such a thing of ego with him. He has his own idea of what a man is, and that doesn't include a son who is gay. It never will."

"Is there anything I can do?" I asked.

"No. Things are the way they are."

I slid closer and put an arm around Meyer's shoulders. "You know it's going to be okay."

"But my parents. They're…."

I had very strong opinions, but Meyer didn't need to hear exactly what I thought of his family at this particular moment. I suspected Meyer also didn't need to hear platitudes and explanations of how things could be worse. "I wish I knew what to say to make you feel better." I smiled. "So, Option A, I can dish your parents from here to eternity, telling you exactly what I think of them and how they aren't good enough for you if they're going to act that way. Option B, I can commiserate with you and tell you that I hope they come around, and that it does get easier."

"Is there an Option C?" Meyer asked, lifting his gaze.

"There's always an Option C. I could quote platitudes to you until you go completely out of your mind and have a breakdown. Then you won't care what happens by the time the men in their clean white coats come to take you away."

A ghost of a smile crossed Meyer's lips. "Thanks for trying to make me feel better. It just might work. Except for the fact that in fifteen minutes, I have to go out there and tape an episode of *Cooking Masters*, acting like there's nothing wrong in front of the other judges, the remaining ten chefs, and, oh, not to mention the entire world."

"Put on your game face and give the performance of your life, one that deserves an Academy Award, or maybe an Emmy, since this is television."

Meyer fake growled. "You're no help at all." He checked the time and lifted Rosco onto the sofa cushion. "I need to get changed before I go on set."

"Me too." Rosco climbed in my lap, and I held him until Meyer left, then hurried to get into my clothes for the taping and out the door without getting covered in cat hair.

"SO FAR our episodes are amazing," Ethan said the following morning at the production meeting. "The chefs are back at their house, and we're going to be bringing them over in an hour, so we have a lot to do. The challenges have been set up and are ready to go, with one addition." Ethan turned to me, and I leaned forward.

"What is it?" Meyer asked.

"It's going to be a surprise for everyone. We want to go off-script to incorporate a little more spontaneity. Just be on your toes and remember to have fun with it."

He went on talking, and I turned to Rachel, who continued to watch Ethan. She knew, I knew she knew, and I immediately tried to think of ways I was going to worm it out of her.

After the meeting broke up, I headed to makeup, sitting next to Meyer, who since our talk had been stoic and largely quiet. That was never a good thing.

I knew what was wrong, and I also knew Meyer would stew it over in his head, chewing on it until there was nothing left. And only then would he actually let whatever was bothering him really drive him crazy. I had seen it before, and I knew Meyer had a tender heart. It was why he kept it locked away and guarded so closely.

I finished first and went to prepare myself, keeping Rosco away from me, then hurried out to the set. I was hosting the appetizer with our guest chef, the previous series winner, Lyle Bolton.

"I hear you have a real sense of humor," Lyle said. The guy was very uptight. He glanced from side to side. "Don't you dare upstage me. I know how this works."

I met his gaze with cold stone. "You do? Then you know that I'm here for the season and you only get today." I wagged my eyebrows as Lyle whirled around like a fairy princess and sauntered over to Meyer as though he was God's gift to everyone in the room. I left them to their conversation, which seemed painfully short and ended with Meyer excusing himself, leaving Lyle standing alone on the set.

"Everyone in place," Ethan said. The chefs filed in, and Lyle and I entered the set.

"Chefs, good morning. I'm sure you know Lyle Bolton, the winner of season seven." I was doing the host duties for the first time. "Today's appetizer challenge is one that I can truly say I wished would stay away. But alas, I'm here to judge a mushroom challenge. My hatred of the edible fungus is quite well known, so your task is to make an appetizer that you believe will change my mind. We have filled the pantry with a dozen different mushrooms, and you will have just thirty minutes. And the time starts… now." I stepped back as the chefs raced to get their ingredients. "Is this as much hectic fun as it looks?" I asked Lyle.

He turned to me, his eyes a little wide, and hesitated. "Yes," he finally answered. "I loved my time on *Cooking Masters*. Each challenge is unique and requires skill and timing." He took a deep breath as we continued talking. "What do you think would endear a mushroom dish to you?"

"I hate the usual texture. So probably a way to make them firm, give them some body, and probably cut down on the deep, earthy taste. That always reminds me of dirt."

Lyle chuckled. "I can see this is going to be a real test for the chef's abilities. Are you sure you're up to tasting all the dishes?"

The little shit. Casting shade right here in the kitchen.

"Definitely. My entire family loves mushrooms, so I've been trying to like them for years. Maybe someone here will be able to change my mind." I kept the conversation light. Even though Lyle was trying to be a pain, it wasn't going to work. I turned to the room. "The winning chef will get an advantage in the next round, and the chef and dish will be featured on my blog as the only mushroom recipe I have ever willingly eaten." That was going to get them plenty of exposure.

Excitement ramped up in the room. Lyle and I continued talking for a few minutes and then stood back because the chefs were now the stars of the show. One woman ran behind the others, nearly colliding with Peter, a blond god whose smile lit up a room. From what I had seen of him, the cameras loved him, and I'd bet the audience was going to be disappointed once he was eliminated. He was a good chef, but not top tier, and unless he grew quickly, he was eventually going home.

"Five minutes. You need to start plating," I called out. "What were these last few minutes of a challenge like for you?" I asked Lyle.

"Completely nerve-wracking. Each chef wants everything to be hot and fresh on the plate, so we put off plating as long as we can. There's also a ton of things to pull together, because we almost always bite off more than we can chew, especially in these quick challenges." He seemed more relaxed and less snippy.

The entire room was filled with the earthy scent of mushrooms, and I did my best to keep the revulsion off my face. It had nothing to do with their dishes and everything to do with me and foods I didn't like.

"Time is up," I said.

The chefs all stepped back. Lyle and I waited for them to get into place and then made our rounds of the room. I approached the first dish with trepidation, and it was about as mushroomy as it looked. Lyle praised the dish, and I took a small bite.

"I want to remind you that the challenge was to make a mushroom dish that I could like." I smiled at her but couldn't stop the shudder that went through me. All the chefs muttered, and I thanked her and moved on.

The next dish was just as bad, and though I somehow managed to swallow my bite, there was no way in hell I was going to get through ten of these dishes without gagging.

"Good morning, chefs," Meyer called as he entered the kitchen. "I think Luke is having a little trouble with your dishes, so I'm going to taste them with Lyle, and we'll present the three that we think he'll like."

I was never so grateful for a save in my life. Looking down the tables, there was no way in hell that I wasn't going to end up being sick.

Meyer and Lyle began at the beginning again, speaking about each dish. I figured my little gaffe would be edited out, but I still hated that I couldn't get through it all.

"Which three do you think Luke might like?" Meyer asked Lyle, and they conferred and asked me to taste the three top dishes. Needless to say, the first two were not among the offerings, though the third contestant, Katy's, was, and it was tasty. There was mushroom flavor, but it wasn't overpowering, and the texture was firm. It helped that she had served the dish on toast, so it was crunchy, with garlic and even a hint of heat.

"This is definitely the winner, and I can tell you that I will eat this again," I said with a smile, and shook Katy's hand. "A mushroom dish I can eat. You will definitely have to show me how to make it." I thanked Meyer and Lyle, as well as the chefs.

Ethan said cut, and everyone relaxed. "We're going to take ten to clean up the kitchen and reset the cameras."

We stepped out of the way, and Lyle stayed to himself. "That guy is a real winner," Meyer said sarcastically, rolling his eyes.

"Yeah, well. He thinks he's all that." I sighed. "Thanks for coming to my rescue. There was no way I was going to make it through all those dishes without getting sick."

"Hey. I'll support you." The warmth in his eyes and the gentle set of his lips sent a rush of heat down my back and right to my groin. I hoped to hell the excitement didn't show.

Rachel strode across the set and over to where we stood. "You two need to be more careful," she whispered.

I cleared my expression, and Meyer turned to her in innocent bemusement.

She leaned closer. "The way you were looking at each other, I'd swear the two of you were on the menu. If you've decided to kindle some flames between you, for God's sake do it, but be fucking careful. Ethan isn't going to stand for anything that might be a controversy or a hint of scandal on his highly respected show." She smiled and turned to where Lyle was speaking with Ethan. "And beware of that one. He's a real backstabbing little bitch."

Damn, the way she could say those words without losing an ounce of radiance from her smile was impressive.

I remembered Ethan's little enigmatic talk and nodded. This set was turning into a pressure cooker, and none of the stoves was even on at the moment.

"Chefs, in keeping with our theme of the day, tonight we will be having a fish fest. Each of you is to make one plated fish dish. Now, the plating is going to be particularly specific. We will be having a special guest at dinner, so in addition to a plate for your judges, you must make an exact replica of your dish in miniature." Rachel held up a bread plate. "Good luck to all of you." She went to leave and then stopped in dramatic fashion. "Katy, you get to assign the fish that each person is going to cook." Rachel oversaw each of the cuts of fish going to the selected chef and then wished them all good luck again.

The chefs were escorted out of the room for their planning session as a team of people moved in to clean the kitchen. We got out of the way and joined Rachel off to the side.

"This is the surprise?" Meyer asked. "Who are we feeding, a kid?"

Rachel pursed her lips. "I'm not saying a word." She was really having fun with this.

"We are going to have to eat again in a few hours?" I asked, shaking my head. My poor belly was not at all ready. "On TV you all make it seem like so much time has passed."

"I know. But with taping, we have to get ahead of the viewing schedule, and they have us really pushing it. I spoke with Ethan, and he said that next week we'll be able to go back to a more normal shooting schedule since we've done so well." She seemed relieved. "Go and relax a while," she told me. "Meyer and I need to check on our chefs." The two of them left the greenroom, and I returned to my trailer, still wondering what was going on with Meyer and when I would be able to talk to him.

I RETURNED to the set a few minutes early. The kitchen was bustling, with Meyer busy overseeing the dishes. He saw me in the wings and came over when he could, directing me out of camera and microphone range.

"I wanted to know how you were holding up."

"I'm okay. Trying not to think about it."

"Come to the apartment tonight and I'll listen," I offered, and Meyer nodded, then excused himself as he returned to give final instructions to the chefs. I went to the dining area, where a large table had been set up for just the four of us. Lyle was already there, but I didn't talk to him, instead taking my time to psych myself up for the gustatory ordeal ahead.

Justin came in from the wings, carrying an animal carrier, and I knew the plaintive sound coming from inside.

"What are you doing with Rosco?" I asked, hurrying over to rescue my friend from his incarceration. He settled in my arms, glaring at Justin.

Rachel breezed in. "Luke, can you come in here and bring Rosco?"

"Why?" Then it hit me. The fish, the small plates. "You have to be kidding me."

"Nope. Rosco is going to get to eat well today." She beckoned, and I figured this had to be a first—a cat as judge on a cooking show.

We entered the kitchen area. "You all remember Luke, and this is Rosco, his picky cat. We need you all to put the miniature version of your dish on the floor along that line, and the dish the cat chooses will receive five thousand dollars. His decision will not affect our judging, but it will put some cash in one of your pockets."

"Now I've seen everything," one of the chefs commented.

I smiled as I waited until all the dishes were in place and then set Rosco down. I half expected him to run for a corner and hide, but the smells must have been too good to resist. Rosco slowly made his way to the plates, sniffing and stalking before taking a bite of the salmon. Of course I could have told them the outcome—that was Rosco's favorite. I let him eat and then picked him up while Rachel announced the winner.

"Thank you, Luke and Rosco, for your help with judging. Now we'll all head in for the final assessment." Thankfully the cameras cut, and Justin took Rosco, this time smart enough not to try to stuff him into a strange carrier before taking him back to the trailer.

I got to follow a few hours later and found Rosco curled on the sofa, sleeping off his food coma. The trademark shooting schedule and notes for next week were already on the table on the familiar canary-yellow paper. I left them where they were for now, figuring I would look at them first thing Monday. If something was urgent, I'd be called, and as it was, I was ready to start my weekend. Rosco barely woke when I lifted him for the ride home.

"GOOD GOD, that bit with the cat came off as hilarious. Rosco actually seemed to look at each plate before selecting the one he wanted," Meyer said that evening just after he arrived at the apartment. "That whole thing could have gone terribly wrong."

"I don't get it at all," I said.

"I spoke to Rachel, and they're billing the episode as the pickiest eater and his picky pet… or something. She thinks it will be funny and the fans will love it, especially after hearing about Rosco in the previous episodes."

"Are you hungry?" Lord knows I wasn't. The very thought of food made my belly rumble in discontent.

Meyer shook his head. "The food I ate on the show, I ended up throwing up as soon as the taping was over. This whole thing with my parents has me on edge, and Ethan stopped by before I left to give me his little speech about behaving and not causing anything that might mean bad publicity." He sighed and wiped his forehead.

"Hey," I told him, "I'm sorry about your dad and mom, I really am. I feel bad that I encouraged you to talk to them."

"No," Meyer protested. "You were right. Regardless of what they think, I had to let them know who I was. They deserved that, and so did I."

I brought Meyer a bottle of ice-cold, half-frozen water and took one myself, and sat next to him on the sofa. "What can I do?"

"I think I'll take Option A," Meyer whispered.

I needed a second to recall what I'd said earlier in the day. "Ah, well, then. Your family are who they are, but if they can't accept you and love you for the person you are inside, then they should be led to the ninth level of hell and sautéed in a large pan until they're just golden brown, and fed to a demon named Fred. Over and over again until they beg for mercy… and béarnaise sauce." He lifted his gaze and chuckled. "But seriously, you're an adult, and while Mom and Dad are important, you don't need them any longer. You have a life of your own, are successful, and on a national television show. You have amazing restaurants and… well, you have to have friends and…."

Meyer shook his head. "You already have more friends here than I do." He sipped his water. "I was never good at making friends. Already half the crew adores you. They think you're the cat's meow, and they bend over backward for you."

"That's because I'm nice and I ask about them when I can. It doesn't take much to listen." I leaned closer. "And when you have something to hide, it affects everything about you. In the back of your mind, you're always wondering if someone knows or if they have figured out that you might be gay. You remain distant, because if they don't know you well, then they will never figure out who you are. It all goes together." I paused because I was preaching, and I didn't want to go there. He didn't need me talking at him that way. "What do you want to do about your mom and dad? Are you going to go see them when we're done?"

Meyer nodded slowly. "I probably should, even if I get the door closed in my face. At least I can try to talk to them face-to-face."

"Yeah. What about the rest of your family? Are they all in Arkansas or spread out?" I tried to remember and couldn't. I had never met any of them, so they were all just names with no faces.

"They're pretty far-flung. My sister called just before I came over, and she's pretty angry with Mom and Dad. Raelynn was always the rebel of the family. She's also the only other one of us who got out, went to college, and left that small town behind. I don't think she's ever been back for more than a holiday visit, and she can't wait to leave every time. I'll fly in when taping is done, stop by for a day or two, and then leave again." He shrugged. "It might be my last visit."

"Or the best visit you've ever had," I corrected.

Meyer shook his head. "I wish I had your attitude. You can smile when everyone around you is shoveling shit your way. Nothing seems to faze you."

"It does. But being gloomy and depressed doesn't help. I try to be positive." I drank some more water, willing my stomach to settle. "I never want to eat most of those dishes again. They were—" I shivered.

"Actually, they were all pretty good. And you really liked the tuna. It was a difficult decision, but I understand. Today was a tough one for you."

"Can I ask what you want to do going forward?" I had to know what Meyer was thinking.

"I've decided I'm not going to hide anymore. I won't shout that I'm gay from the rooftops, but I won't deny it either."

I figured that was a good start and took Meyer's hand. His fingers were rough, and I rubbed slowly along them, entwining mine with his. "That's a huge step."

"I know. But I don't want to hide any longer. But then Ethan starts in with his cautions and paranoia. He's so worried about any sort of talk."

"It's part of his job to make sure the show is good and comes off perfect. I suppose it could be worse. The producers could be in everyone's hair all the time, asking a million questions."

"They respect and trust Ethan, so that's probably why he's so uptight."

I nodded. "But what I don't understand is why you and I being involved would cause a huge scandal. It isn't like I'm a contestant and could use the relationship to further my chances on the show. I don't get it." Maybe I didn't know enough about the entertainment business to really understand it, but it made no sense to me.

"This is an image business. That's all that matters. No one cares how anything truly is, only how it looks. So if it looks like something is wrong, then it is. The contestants could complain that either you or I could be influencing the other, though I doubt that would get them very far. Still, someone might make a stink, and then *that's* what they're talking about, rather than the current season and the onscreen drama. Studios and networks can control the onscreen drama, but the rest… well, they basically hate what they can't control." Meyer set down his water, yawning as he leaned back in the chair.

"God, I'm glad this condensed schedule is over. It's killing us all." I yawned because Meyer's was contagious.

"Yeah, well, Ethan is asking that we come back tomorrow to shoot some takes that didn't come out. It shouldn't be too bad, but he needs the footage, and then on Tuesday, we head to the desert for an episode."

I was already so tired. When I had agreed to this, I had no idea how hard it was going to be. I was never a stranger to work, but this was draining on so many levels, and I wasn't quite sure how much longer I was going to be able to keep up this pace. I really needed a break.

"Is there anything on the schedule for the weekend?"

"No. I thought if you wanted, we could go to the beach or Disneyland. Do something fun, something that doesn't require cameras or instructions. And maybe you and I could cook together. We haven't done that in a long time."

That sounded like a lot of fun. I had come all this way, so it would be nice to see something of the city while I was here. "Let's figure it out later when I can think." I closed my eyes as fatigue washed over me. It was lucky that I had planned ahead and a number of blog posts were all set to go, because by rights I should be putting some together, but I didn't have the energy.

I felt rather than saw Meyer draw nearer, heat rising around me even though Meyer didn't actually touch me at first. His lips brushed over mine and passion rose, but I was too tired to move.

"Meyer, the spirit is willing." God, was it ever—I wanted him badly. It was sexy knowing that he'd told his parents about himself, because part of me knew that Meyer had taken that chance for me. Before, I hadn't felt like Meyer cared enough, and now it seemed that he did. Although I did hope he hadn't told them only because of me. Anyway, my mind snapped back to the here and now as Meyer kissed me again. "But the body…." I had to be honest. Even for him, I didn't want to move.

"Then maybe I should go and let you rest."

I didn't want him to go, and I managed to slide my eyes open. "Let's just go to bed. I can't eat anything more."

"Then finish your water so you stay hydrated." Meyer handed me the bottle, and I took it, drinking absently.

He left the room, and I didn't even think about where he'd gone before the lights in the room clicked off and he tugged me to my feet. Meyer guided me into the bedroom and slowly began stripping me out of my clothes. That should have been the prelude to sex, and I did try, but there wasn't enough willpower in the world to make anything happen. Meyer got me in the bed and pulled up the covers. I rolled over, closing my eyes.

I don't know why I expected Meyer to leave. Maybe it was because when we were together before, if sex wasn't on the table, he usually left to protect his secret. That was the reason he gave, but I'd always thought that maybe I wasn't good enough or that I wasn't *enough* for him. So when he slid under the covers, cuddling right against me in the heavily air-conditioned room, I sighed and smiled. "That's nice."

"Go to sleep. We'll talk in the morning." Meyer slid his arms around my belly, and I shut my eyes, falling to sleep almost instantly.

WHEN I woke, it was still dark. I was on my back and… oh God….

"Meyer," I gasped. Hell, I'd thought I was having this marvelous dream, and instead it was true. Meyer slid his lips down over my shaft, and I groaned, pressing my hips upward for more, still half-asleep, the clouds of drowsiness intensifying the sensation. And when Meyer's fingers slid up my chest to lightly pinch my nipple, I hissed and quivered. Not quite pain, but adding incredibly to the intensity.

He didn't say anything but took me deeper instead. My head swam, and I sat up, needing to watch Meyer as he drove me to nirvana. I flopped my head back, giving up trying to see in the darkness and just felt, letting Meyer take me where he wanted to go. And, man, it was one hell of a journey. He brought me high, let me hang there, right on the near-screaming edge, and then backed off, only to do it again and again until control was lost, and I was fully in his hands—or actually, his lips. Then, just as I couldn't take any more, Meyer finished me off, and I tumbled into sweet oblivion, flopping back breathlessly on the bed.

"Give… me a minute and…," I gasped.

Meyer chuckled and slipped out of the bed. He returned and climbed in next to me, his hands a little damp. "I'm good, honey. You took me right along with you." He held me, and I drifted back to sleep in a haze of warmth and care.

I could very easily get used to this, and I wanted to. But things had gone wrong before, and I wasn't ready to go all in the way I had in the past. Call me wary, smart, or just once-burned, but I was going to need to see if this was real. But, damn, I was starting to really want it to be.

CHAPTER 8

"DO YOU really want to go to Disneyland?" Meyer asked that weekend as we zoomed down the freeway in his smooth ride.

"Sure. I never got to go as a kid. We could never afford the trip to Florida or California, and the entrance fees, hotel, and all that. Mom and Dad always said that they weren't interested and that we didn't have the money for it whenever I asked, so I stopped asking."

"Okay, then." Meyer made the turn onto the I-5 South, and we ground through the city traffic toward Anaheim. "I took my nieces when they came to visit last year, and I have the Disney app on my phone. Go ahead and buy two tickets, then set up the FASTPASS for the rides that you want."

I figured out the app and was able to make the purchases. "What rides do you like?"

"Get the big ones that you can. It's tempting to get Pirates or the Haunted Mansion, but those lines go really quickly. Just pick the ones you think you'll like, and we'll go for it. Research the rides and have fun."

I did my best and finished up as we pulled into the parking lot. I was excited, and the day didn't disappoint. Meyer was a blast to be with. We got colorful MagicBands, his green and mine yellow, went on every ride, and when we got off, Meyer was just like a kid. I got some basic pins, and we traded them for some pretty cool ones with various Disney cast members. For a day, I could imagine what it was like to be a kid again.

"This is completely silly and so much fun," I told Meyer as we got a Mickey ice cream bar. "Maybe a churro later," I said, taking my first bite.

"You're like a damn kid, and I love it. After the food, I'd say the teacups are out, but we should get in line for the Matterhorn. It's a classic, and I love that ride."

"I knew you would," I told Meyer. "That's why I FASTPASSed it. We need to be there in ten minutes." I grinned, and Meyer bumped my shoulder with a warm smile. I knew he liked coasters, but the fun, interesting ones, not the big scary ones. "We can start walking that direction, finish eating, and then get in line."

This really was the happiest place on earth, and I could certainly attest to that. Today did indeed feel like something out of a fantasy.

I drew closer as I finished my ice cream and half leaned my head against his shoulder. Meyer stiffened for a second and then relaxed. I pulled away, knowing instantly that I had crossed a line Meyer wasn't comfortable with yet.

Meyer was quiet for a minute, and I knew I had added tension between us. Thankfully, it dissipated once we reached the attraction and entered the line at our appointed time. "I always loved this ride." He had said it before, but Meyer was trying to break the silence between us.

"I remember watching some of the reruns of the old Disney specials when I was a kid, and I wanted to come here. I can't remember how many times I asked Mom and Dad to bring me." Of course, it had been futile, as were all things they weren't interested in. As I got older, I found out that it wasn't Mom so much as my father. He was as tight as a witch's ass and didn't spend anything he didn't have to. Vacations were a waste of money if he had to stay in a hotel, so the only ones we ever got to go on were the kind where we could stay with family and friends. I also found out that after spending a week with my dad, their friends drifted away and weren't so friendly any longer.

We scanned our bands, walked to the front, and boarded our bobsled pretty fast. "I'm ready for fun," Meyer yelled like an excited kid, and I smiled as I held on, the sled lifting toward the top of the ride, which zigged, zagged, and zoomed, over all too soon, and then we were getting off and on our way to the next attraction.

There were many things I found I loved about Disney, and one of them was the park after dark, with all the lights, kids carrying balloons that blinked, and the lighted parade. It was magical and exciting, but what excited me more was when Meyer suggested that as soon as the parade started, we head somewhere else. I loved a parade as well as anyone else, but skipping it was a chance to avoid the crowds. The Haunted Mansion and other rides were deserted, spooks danced all around us, time and time again, before we left and had a pirate adventure.

By the time the park closed, we were worn out with fun, and Meyer drove me home. The two of us tumbled into the apartment, still laughing, with Rosco scolding until I fed him, even though he had plenty of food and was just pissed that I hadn't been home all day. He stayed away as Meyer damned near made me scream like on one of those coasters, but with a very different, much more intimate sensation. Once we quieted, Rosco jumped on the bed and kneaded himself a space right near my feet before curling up to go to sleep, just like I did, only I was content to be held in Meyer's arms.

The thing was, I could really get used to this. Meyer was familiar but exciting, and in my experience, that was a very rare combination.

I WOKE in the morning to sweet carried on the scent of coffee. I didn't even know that there had been the ingredients in the apartment, but Meyer lured me out of bed with the scent of cinnamon rolls in the oven. I was alone in bed, so I got up and found Rosco curled up on the seat of one of the kitchen chairs, watching Meyer. It seemed Rosco had forgiven Meyer for his past transgressions. Or possibly my cat now associated Meyer with food. Either way, Rosco glared at me when I eyed his chair, and blinked and lowered his head rather than getting up off his perch.

"I thought we could go to the store today, maybe get a little lunch later, and for dinner I was thinking a Caesar salad, pasta with carbonara, and I can make a tiramisu for dessert."

"Are you trying to spoil me?" I asked. Meyer knew my favorites, and he'd listed three of them.

"Maybe a little."

It sounded like a quiet day—at least I hoped it would be—and I could use one of those. "I have to write a blog post today so I can stay out ahead of the curve. And I should do the winner's post. Katy sent me the instructions for her winning mushroom dish, and I should get it written. I can save it and schedule it to post right after the episode airs." I blinked and sighed, utterly content, especially when Meyer kissed me.

MONDAY MORNING, Meyer went home early. He said he needed to change, and that was undoubtedly part of it, but I was pretty sure he was also a little wary of being seen arriving on the set with me. After the mysterious stuff Ethan had told me, and assuming Meyer had gotten the same talk, I didn't really blame him.

Felix talked almost the entire trip, and I engaged in conversation as best I could. But my mind was elsewhere, and I needed to get in to look at the schedule so I would know what was expected of me today. Felix dropped me at my trailer before seven, and I went inside and snatched up the timetable from the table. I blinked more than once as I read the words scrawled on the inside of the sheet.

I know your secret, and unless you want everything about your personal life sprawled over the entertainment pages, you need to pay attention.

I turned to Rosco, who was already setting himself up in his favorite perch. The damned cat just blinked back at me and was no help at all.

"Like I have any secrets." I had never made any bones about being gay. But I wasn't stupid and had a pretty clear idea that whoever wrote this note had no idea about that. "Don't you just hate a blackmailer who doesn't do his homework?"

Then a thought occurred to me: Rosco knew who had put this in my trailer, and the cat wasn't saying a thing.

Rosco meowed his agreement, and I put the page in my bag and made sure he had food and water before heading out to makeup and wardrobe, where I caught up with Meyer. He seemed normal, so apparently I had been singled out by this particular letter writer.

I waited until Meyer was alone and told him he needed to come to the trailer. I was not going to talk about this little missive out in the open for fear that someone would overhear.

"I have to be on set in ten minutes," Meyer told me, and I needed to as well. There was nothing to be gained by telling him now and upsetting Meyer before a long day of shooting, so I put the note on the back burner, psyched myself up, and prepared for whatever contests they decided to torture me with this time.

"OKAY," MEYER said as we left the set for the final time at the end of the day. The chefs were as exhausted as I was, and the following day everyone was heading out into the desert for the elimination challenge. I was pretty sure I knew what they were going to have to be doing, and it was something few of them had ever done before, that was for certain. "You needed to speak with me earlier when things were way too busy?"

"Yeah. By the way, do you keep your trailer locked?" I asked.

Meyer scoffed. "Always. I hate it when people are in and out. Why?"

I led the way across the area to my trailer, glanced around, then unlocked it and stepped inside. There were no new notes, which was good, and Rosco purred as he hurried over for some attention. "Did you keep the bad guys away?" I asked, and gave him a treat from the container. I opened my attaché, pulled out the note, and handed it to Meyer. "Don't freak out." Of course, that was everybody's cue to do just that. "This was on my table when I left on Friday. I thought it was a schedule and I didn't look at it until this morning." I handed him the page, and Meyer went stark white.

"Is this a joke?" he rasped, then coughed like he'd swallowed his tongue.

"I wish it was." I tried not to smile. "Though I can't really think what kind of secrets this person thinks I have. I haven't kept it a secret that I'm gay, and in fact, I have discussed briefly the meals I've had with my dates on the blog. I don't make a huge deal out of it, but my loyal followers know that I don't swing in a straight line." I tried to add a little lightness, but it fell flat, so I cleared my throat. "You always keep your trailer locked and closed up, so it's possible that this guy had notes for both of us. I leave mine open because Justin comes in here to look in on Rosco during the day. So I can see how someone was able to leave the note, but does anyone really think I'm going to pay to keep the fact that I'm gay quiet? This is cable TV. We have gay chefs on this particular season." I shrugged. I didn't want to think that Justin would do something like this, but he was the first person who came to mind because of his access to just about everything. I hated that I even thought of it and did my best to push the idea away.

"Holy fuck," Meyer breathed, and practically jumped up. "I should go." He reached for the door, and I leveled my gaze at him with the force of a boulder rolling downhill.

"If you go barreling out of here like some Meyer-in-a-box, someone is going to think you and I are doing something wrong, and we aren't." I didn't look away. "Are we, Meyer?" I pressed. This was a decision point for him. I knew what he'd already said, but he was going to have to decide the kind of person he wanted to be, and I needed to know if he was someone I could trust when the shit hit the fan. And if not…. I knew this wasn't the best timing, but we never get to choose that. Life has a way of throwing crap at you, and it was how you dealt with it that counted.

Meyer paused, then finally said, "Okay. So what do we do from here?" His hand shook, but he stayed where he was.

"Nothing at all. Watch a little, but don't say anything, and act as though nothing has happened. I expect our note writer wants to stir up some drama, so we aren't going to give them any."

"Okay. But what if this note has nothing to do with you and me? What other secrets do you have?" Now it was Meyer's turn to try the stare. It didn't work. I had always been the one who could stare him down. Meyer tried it, but didn't affect me, much to my delight.

I laughed. "What sort of secrets could I have? I live in a small apartment with my cat, I write a blog, and I work." I thought a second. "Occasionally I go out with friends, and I have an assistant with a much more interesting life than my own. Call the tabloids and alert *Entertainment Tonight*." I rolled my eyes. "There is nothing about me that is scandalworthy in the least. So all we can do is wait for whoever this is to show his or her hand. Let them hang themselves, so to speak." As I called Felix for a ride, Rosco ambled over and deigned to be picked up. "I'm going to go to the apartment and try to sleep for a while."

"Yeah. I should go too. Tomorrow is going to be hot as hell, so drink lots of water before you leave the house, and wear light, flowing clothes and no dark colors—otherwise you'll roast." He stepped a little closer. "I'll try not to worry, but please be really careful."

The curtains were pulled, so I gave him a light kiss. "You too. I'll see you on location tomorrow." I really wasn't too concerned. What in the heck could someone think they had on me?

Meyer left the trailer, and I came out with Rosco in my arms right afterward, locked the door, and slid into the back seat of the car. Rosco stayed on the floor, lying low as Felix drove us home.

"Are things going well?" Felix asked.

"I think so. This is my first television show, but it seems to be going okay. We're back on schedule, and everyone seems relieved about that. Tomorrow we're on location in the desert." I fished in my pocket and found the schedule with the location. I passed it up to him. "I'll need to be there by seven. They are hoping to start early. What time will we need to leave?"

He read the paper. "Out there?" he asked. "I'll pick you up before five so we'll miss most of the traffic. That should get us there in plenty of time."

"Thank you." I closed my eyes and let him drive, trying to relax, but that damned note kept running through my mind, along with the openmouthed shock and pale skin of abject fear that Meyer had expressed whether he'd meant to or not. Just when I thought things with Meyer could possibly be on an even keel, I was pretty sure that the note was going to scare him away. I also needed to figure out who was behind this, though I had no idea where to start.

I SLEPT much of the way into the desert. It was still dark and the ride was smooth, so I took advantage. Felix seemed content with his own thoughts, and I let myself descend into mine. This entire thing with the note had me wondering just who we were dealing with. It had to be someone no one would think twice about seeing go into my trailer. Though they could have snuck in, there were so many people around that it would be nearly impossible not to be seen. So hiding in plain sight was logical.

That got me running through each crew member, as well as the others I'd been working with. Some of those people I was starting to think of as friends, and now suspicion crept in… and I hated it. I hated the way it made me question each and every person, from the lady who did my makeup and chatted with me each day, to the wardrobe manager who made sure I was impeccably dressed. I had even decided to leave Rosco at home that day just so I wouldn't need Justin to come into the trailer to feed and water him. I was fucking changing the way I lived because of that note, and maybe that was the most insidious thing of all.

The sun rose as we crossed out of the mountains, and the desert stretched in front of me. I had heard that it had a beauty all its own, and maybe it did, but what I saw was various shades of brown on top of brown. Still, the hills stretched and rolled over the land, and Felix stayed quiet, so I took the chance to look.

"It's not too much farther."

"Thanks, Felix. Do you know how the chefs are getting here?" I asked. I wasn't sure how much he was in the loop on anything.

"They were driven out to within a mile of the location, and they're going to be coming in on donkeys." He snickered. "I would love to see that."

"Then why don't you stay around here and watch? I'm going to need you to drive me back, and going all that way only to have to come back again doesn't make any sense at all." We shared a smile via the rearview mirror.

The light increased, and we made a turn off the main highway, traveling down a barely kept road to a small tent encampment. "Is this it?" The place sure didn't look like much. I saw Meyer, Ethan, and a number of the other crew, so this had to be it. The entire place was sunbaked and looked like something out of sheer hell. I got out and joined the others under one of the large canopy tents, where misters and fans had been set up to try to cool the place. It didn't seem to be working to me, and I hoped I didn't melt into a puddle of goop on the ground.

A wall of heat assailed me with the force of a punch to the gut. Sweat broke out instantly, with the shade and fans providing minimal relief from the blast-furnace heat.

"Go to makeup and get yourself ready," Ethan told me right away. "I want to get this sequence wrapped up as quickly as possible so we can get back to civilization and air-conditioning."

There was none of the usual pep in his step as he went to make sure the cameras were set up the way he wanted them.

I managed to sit in the makeup chair and not have the stuff run all down my face. They used very little, and for that I was real grateful.

"Hey, did you hear?" Darlene said once I was nearly done. She took a step back to check her work and then had me lift my face slightly. "Apparently there's a rumor going around the crew that a judge is having a thing… with one of the contestants." She rolled her eyes. "Like that would happen. Ethan would scope out any of that hanky-panky so fast, their heads would roll."

"No way," I agreed. "Why would anyone do that? The chef would be booted off the show in an instant, and the judge would never be able to work again." It seemed really stupid, and yet my head went back to that damned note. Did whoever sent it think that I was the judge? That was about as stupid a thing as possible, but it would explain the note and why it was worded so strangely.

"I don't believe it either. There are cameras and people in that house of theirs almost all the time. The only time that people don't watch them is when they're asleep or in the bathroom." Darlene seemed amused by that. "Not that I'd want anyone that close up in my business."

I had to agree with her. "Let me know if you hear anything more. I suppose on a show with a crew like this, rumors fly all over the place."

Darlene leaned closer. "Sweetheart, you got dropped right in the middle of *Melrose Place* and you had no idea at all." She turned me around so I could look into the mirror. "You look gorgeous, as usual. Just don't touch your face. In this heat, you'll smear so danged easily. Have fun out there."

"Thanks." I took off the clothes protectors and threw them away before heading to wardrobe and then on to find the rest of the cast. "So, what exactly is the challenge?" I asked as I looked around the area already set up for cooking. Then I got it. "Reflector ovens," I said, remembering my Boy Scout training. And danged if they didn't look exactly like the one I had made as a kid, with reflective aluminum concentrating the heat of the sun.

"Precisely," Rachel said. "But each chef has to make one hot and one cold dish, so they are going to have to manage both resources out here." That was going to be difficult at best, but something cold was going to taste amazing in this heat, as long as it truly was cold. "They'll have a limited pantry and will have to win their protein. Plenty of strategy and creativity." She dabbed her face with a tissue and leaned back in her chair to catch the breeze off one of the fans that was blowing the misted air. Mostly those things did very little to ease the discomfort level, so I did my best not to move, even when Meyer sat next to me.

"Any more notes?" he whispered, and I shook my head before explaining about the rumor that was going around. "I heard something like that as well."

I didn't know where it started, but it wasn't good at all. I knew I wasn't involved with anyone other than Meyer, and I was sure that the reverse was true. Rachel hardly seemed like the type to have something going on with anyone on the show. She was too professional.

"So what gives?"

I shrugged. "You know how rumors get started. Someone says something, and suddenly it's all blown out of proportion. I think this is just talk and will blow over." Movement, even talking, just made me hotter, so I sat still. "This whole thing is just stupid."

"Okay. The chefs will be arriving soon, so everyone needs to be in their places for when they get here."

One of the production assistants hurried out toward an enclosure with a cooler and set it on the table. Meyer and I stood just in the shade off to the side so we could see what was going on. Rachel was supposed to meet them and explain the challenge, but she was looking more and more like a wet rag.

"Are you okay?" I called for some water and handed her a sweating bottle that seemed to dry in my hand. I passed it to her, and she drank most of it. "Does that help?"

"Oh God, yes," she whispered.

I got her a chair and let her sit. "You need to take it easy in this heat," I explained, and she nodded.

"I'm trying, but the shit follows me wherever I go. I had asked them to bring my trailer because it has air-conditioning, but they said we were only going to be here for the day and it was too much to bring along." She swore under her breath. "Next time I'm going to have my agent put it in my contract." She flashed a smile and drank some more water. "That's better." She drained the last of the bottle and stood slowly. "Here they come. It's time to go to work." She stepped out into the sun, with cameras following her to meet the chefs as they arrived.

I got out of the way, returning to my small area, where a chair and table had been set up. I sat down, picking up the production schedule warily, but the canary-yellow paper was as it should be. Still, I looked around to see if I was being watched, read through the updated schedule, and set it aside, taking a few quiet moments before I was needed.

Rachel sat down in the other chair, fanning herself, seemingly thankful that Meyer and their guest judge, who had written a cookbook on using these type of reflector ovens, were going around to talk to each of the chefs. I was a little redundant at the moment and wondered if I was even needed out here at all. But apparently a table was being set up under a tent for judging, about fifty feet away so it appeared to be out in the desert all by itself. I wandered over to check it out and wished I hadn't, the sun beating down on me. By the time I returned, so had Meyer and the guest judge. He introduced himself as Gerald Hines and wilted into a different seat as we all tried to stay out of the heat.

"I'm worried one of the chefs is going to pass out."

"They have plenty of water and only an hour to cook, so they won't be out there too long, but it is the challenge, to use the sun to prepare the meal—nothing electric or powered, just themselves and nature. I have used these ovens in front of a fire when I was a Scout and thought it would be a very eco-friendly way of preparing food, especially out here in the intense sun." Gerald was clearly excited about the idea, even if the heat deflated him a little.

"I used them when I was a kid, once or twice. They were a curiosity then, but I can see the practicality out here." I turned to watch the chefs as best I could. "How do you think they're doing?"

"I think the cold portion of the cook-off is going to be the real challenge. They only have ice, and it isn't going to last very long in this heat."

One of the runners came by and handed out yet another updated schedule. I reviewed it and set it on the table, committing it to memory. I was going to be needed at the table in about half an hour.

"Do you cook in the desert a lot?" I asked Gerald.

"I have, but not for a contest like this."

We grew quiet as the time wound down. Rachel led us to the table, where the four of us sat under a flowing white canopy that kept away much of the direct sun. The chefs brought over their dishes, and we sampled each of them. It wasn't until I was done and the chargers that we had used under the settings—as well as to help weight the tablecloth—were lifted that I saw the page under it. I grabbed the piece of paper and slipped it into my pocket. No one seemed to notice, and I did my best not to make a big deal out of it.

The four judges all agreed to meet back in LA to discuss what we had eaten, and the crew was already packing up to get the hell out of the heat.

"Do you, Gerald, or Rachel need a ride?" I asked.

Meyer apparently had ridden out with Ethan and was grateful for the lift back to the city. Rachel and Gerald had rides, so Meyer and I got in the back of the car, the air-conditioning blasting on full.

"Thank God. I swear I'm wet in places I have never sweated before." He leaned back, and I waited until we were on the road toward LA before pulling the paper from my pocket. "What's that?"

"It was under my charger." I opened what was definitely another of those notes. This one said much the same thing as the first, but there was one very important difference: it was addressed to Rachel.

"What the hell?" I showed it to Meyer. "Do you think the other one was supposed to go to her and instead it got put in my trailer?" This was looking like a comedy of errors.

Meyer shook his head and showed me his letter. Damn, it said nearly the same thing. "What do you make of this? It was among my production notes."

"Someone is trying to stir up drama." That was the only reasonable explanation I could come up with. "A member of the crew must have gotten the idea to have a little fun and see what they could shake up." And I'd just remembered who had been setting up the table for us. I didn't want to think that Justin was behind this, but I had seen him there making sure that everything was all set up. So he could have put the note under the plate, thinking it was Rachel's. I kept my suspicion to myself because I didn't want to hurt an innocent person, but I was going to have to keep a close eye out.

"But why?" Meyer asked.

"Attention," Felix said, and I had to agree with him. "Everyone in this town wants their fifteen minutes of fame, and if they can stir up trouble and uncover secrets…." He let the rest sink in unsaid.

"Ethan needs to be aware of this," Meyer said.

"I agree, but what if he's getting them too? He's been edgy and snappy as hell for days. I'm willing to bet that we're all getting them in one form or another, and the asshole behind all of this is just sitting back to see who reacts. Hell, maybe they're following some of us to see what they can dig up." I shook my head. "This really isn't normal."

"Nope. I've done a number of shows, and usually everyone gets along pretty well. We all have a common goal, so working together is pretty seamless. But shit like this makes the entire process a struggle." Meyer grinned as though he'd just come up with something brilliant. "What if that's the plan? What if strife and confusion is what they're going for, to disrupt the show and maybe get it canceled?"

Now that was something I hadn't thought of. "I kind of doubt that. This is the eighth season, and it has a great following. I know that as the seasons go on, interest can wane, but that doesn't seem to be the case as far as I can tell. A lot of people still watch, and as long as the show is kept interesting and fresh, there shouldn't be a problem."

"Except if there are enough rumors and scandal, there will be people picketing the network. Two seasons ago, one of the judges was touched by all that sex abuse going on. He didn't have anything to do with it, but someone on one of his previous shows on the network did. There were letter-writing campaigns and pickets to get him removed from the show because somehow he should have known and stopped it. I don't know if he could or couldn't have," Meyer explained. "The association was enough to taint him... well, that and a few vocal people who had it in for him and used this as an excuse." He shook his head. "I don't think abuse is right in any form, but giving someone grief because they worked in a kitchen where the chef was accused of it is something completely different. Still, Hollywood is weird at the moment, and there has been plenty of self-reflection and a fear of scandal that's bone-deep." Meyer leaned back.

"Okay, but what do we do?"

Meyer humphed a second. "There's nothing we can do, except try to figure out who is stirring the pot and then try to find a way to stir things back the other way."

What I really wanted to ask was what effect this had on us. Meyer had surprised me so far, but I really wasn't expecting that to continue. As the pressure mounted for everything and everyone to look and be as aboveboard and rumor-free as possible, I expected that I would become one of the casualties. Which sucked.

"Do you want Felix to drop you at the studio? Is that where you left your car?"

"Yes," Meyer answered, and I tapped my foot nervously, hoping for some other indication of what Meyer intended to do, but he sat quietly. I sighed, figuring I wasn't going to get anything more.

At the studio, we dropped off Meyer before Felix drove me to the apartment. I went up, showered immediately, fed Rosco, and changed his litter. Then I sat on the sofa with Rosco on my lap, stroking his fur. He seemed to know I needed company and was more than willing to provide it. He purred just before the knock on the door, and I got up to see who it was.

"I wasn't expecting you," I told Meyer, who kissed me as soon as the door was closed.

"I didn't want to talk about things in the car." He cupped my cheeks and kissed me again. "I think you and I need to talk."

I knew what that could mean, and it was rarely good. There were so many times in my life when that exact phrase had been used as a prelude to bad news that I couldn't help tensing, even though I wanted to keep cool. If Meyer wanted to take a step back, then I would deal with it.

"Okay." I held my breath as I sat back down, then released it when Rosco climbed onto my lap, purring and rubbing against me. "I know," I whispered, and stroked his back. Rosco was always comforting, and that was a joy.

"I just think that you and I need to talk to each other. It was something we were shit at in the past. I thought you understood me and figured you wanted the same things I did, and it turned out we were both wrong, and you got hurt." Meyer sat down next to me. "I don't want that to happen again."

That was most definitely a switch. "I don't particularly relish getting hurt either, but I don't really see a way out of it. The fact is that I'm not going to stay here after the show is done. Rosco and I will get on a plane and go home. You will have your life and your restaurants here. The other thing is that you're figuring out who you are and what you want. Believe me, there is a whole different world out there for you to experience now that you've opened the closet door."

"I'm well aware of that world outside, thank you very much," Meyer quipped. "What I'm saying is that I'm older, hopefully wiser, and a helluva lot less stupid. I can't have everything my own way… and that was what I wanted before. I always thought that I could keep part of myself quiet and that it was nobody's business who I spent my time with."

I knew the boxes a mind could build to wall off anything unpleasant or what someone didn't want to face.

"I know now that attitude cost me you, and it cost me part of my soul. I want it back. I want *you* back. I want to be whole and…." He paused. "Most of all, I think I want what you want and what you've had all along."

This entire conversation was the last thing I ever expected to hear from Meyer. I wanted to believe it and put faith in it, but the hurt kept me at bay. "Meyer, I can't go back to being a secret—for anyone. That nearly killed me. I had you in part of my life, and the world in another. It tore me apart, and I can't do that again." There was no way that I could split myself in two once more, because this time I wasn't going to be able to put myself back together, at least not nearly as easily.

"You deserve more than to be anyone's secret. Luke, you deserve to be the center of someone's world."

Shit, this really sounded like Meyer was leading up to a breakup. Not that we were exactly together, but that's certainly what it felt like.

I set Rosco on the sofa cushion beside me and got up to go into the kitchen. I got a beer out of the refrigerator, holding it in my hand. "There's no need for you to go into the rest. I get it and it's fine." I huffed as my defenses, the ones I had done a good job of building after the last time I'd gotten that same kind of speech from Meyer, started slipping back into place. "This is something I've heard before."

"What the hell are you talking about?" Meyer asked snippily.

"Oh, come on. I know the 'let them down easy' speech when I hear it. What's next? 'It's not you, it's me'?" I rolled my eyes and opened the beer. "Don't think I didn't know this was coming. I have. Things are getting heated up, and there are people on the set just itching to gather a bunch of secrets. And you have a big one that I'm a threat to expose. I know that. It's only natural that you would want to back away and try to retrench. I get it… I do." I stood in the doorway. "I do understand." And damn it all, I knew I should have stayed away from him. But even now, his eyes threatened to draw me closer when I had to be strong.

"I think you have the wrong idea," Meyer said as he calmly leaned back in the chair, crossing one leg over the other.

"I do?" I lowered my head, flashing my best skeptical expression.

"Yeah, you do." Meyer held out his hand, and I slowly came over. Rosco lifted his head as though checking to make sure I was okay before closing his eyes again.

"Then what is it you want?" Obviously I was crap at figuring things when it came to him.

"Honestly, I'm still figuring things out. I've come to accept some things about myself that are difficult. You know about my family. I was brought up in a small town where everyone acted the same and believed the exact same things. The ones who didn't left because they didn't fit in. I've tried to fit in… I desperately tried."

"And you didn't. That's why you're here, hosting a television show, running your restaurants, and making a huge name for yourself, and they're still sitting on their asses in that small town, doing exactly nothing." I felt my temper rising. "You already did the hard stuff. You got out and made something of yourself. Do you really think your customers are going to care if the person in your life is a man or a woman, as long as you deliver the same stellar food you always have?" I shook my head. "It all comes back to how you want to live your life."

"I'm figuring that out." Meyer leaned forward slightly. "I should have done this years ago. Then we could have had all this time together and had a chance to be happy."

"It wouldn't have worked." I wasn't sure things were going to work between us now, but I was willing to try. "It's easy to blame the failure of things back then on you not being out. But that wasn't all of it. Neither of us was ready for a full-blown, real relationship. You were still keeping parts of yourself a secret, but so was I in a way. I allowed you to treat me as a secret and was content to be this quiet part of your life. I needed to learn to stand up for myself and be the person I was."

Meyer tilted his head slightly in that adorable way he had when he didn't understand something. "I always thought of you as this confident, self-assured person."

"Nope." I chuckled. "People like that don't have relationships like ours. It wasn't until I started the blog that I came to realize the source of my self-consciousness."

"You mean the food thing?" Meyer asked, repositioning to the sofa.

"Yeah. I was picked on because of the things I didn't like that everyone else did. Mom knew I hated bananas, but she bought them every week, and most of the time they were the only fruit in the house because if I got hungry enough, I'd eat them." I was also coming to realize that my mom and dad had a very skewed view of parenthood. "I was picked on because I didn't eat certain foods. I remember when I went to college and could eat, or not eat, anything I wanted... you would think it would be a relief, but it wasn't. I kept expecting to be belittled, and never talked about food. I choked things down because the other guys ate them."

"Hey. It's okay. You will never have to eat anything you don't want to... well, except maybe in the upcoming challenges, but you can make that ick face all you want." Meyer smiled. "If you don't like it, just say so."

"I will. But even there, it's—"

"No," Meyer interrupted. "That comment about not feeding that dish to your cat is going to go viral. The marketing team is already getting memes ready." He held me. Meyer actually put his arms around me and just held me. "They asked you to be here because you're honest about food and what you like. And I should never have tried to teach you to like the things you don't."

I shrugged. "I think you and I got off the track again."

"Maybe we did. But we should be able to talk about what bothers us. And I promise that as long as I get to cook for you, I will never add bananas or mushrooms to your food." He grinned, and I leaned against him. Maybe that was as close to a declaration of love as I could expect right at the moment.

"You know, I'll take that with all the feeling that's intended."

Meyer leaned closer, and I groaned when his lips touched mine, the electric current instantly chasing away any hint of fatigue. Rosco jumped off the sofa with an annoyed *mrrr*, and Meyer pressed me back against the cushions. I didn't have time to think if any of the neighbors could see in through the balcony from the other building, and frankly, at the moment, I didn't care. Maybe they got an eyeful, but the way Meyer kissed down my neck, tugged off my shirt, and then ran his lips over a nipple, frizzed my brain and made rational thought something out of my grasp. Threats, letters, hot-as-hell shooting locations—they all went out of my head as my attention centered on Meyer and how he made me feel alive.

Yeah, in ways I was afraid of him. But not in a physically violent kind of thing. It was more in the fact that Meyer could hurt me again, but hell and blast, the way Meyer pushed me through the need to hibernate and tugged me back into the light of day, the light that meant I could have care and maybe something deep and meaningful in my life, was worth it.

"Meyer...," I groaned. "What are you doing to me?"

"I'm going to make your eyes roll to the back of your head and then, only then, I'll carry you into the bedroom and make love to you for the rest of the night. And tomorrow, when everyone asks you why you have bags under your eyes, you can either tell them the truth or not, but you will know that I was the one who put them there."

The deep, gravelly roughness in Meyer's voice left no doubt that was exactly what he intended to do, and I was more than ready. In fact, I shook like a palm branch in a gale at the very thought of it.

"I BET I know what someone has been doing," Darlene whispered the following morning. "You look like hell, your skin is sallow, and you're seconds from falling asleep in my chair, and yet, damn it all, you're fucking smiling. That can only mean that you got something last night." She winked, and I tried to keep from smirking. It was hard, and I doubted anyone was that good an actor. "Don't worry. It will be our secret." She got to work, and I sat still, letting my mind wander.

"I need all of you in the production office," Ethan barked.

"What crawled up his butt and died?" I asked once Ethan had stormed out.

"Didn't you watch *E! News* last night?" Darlene asked, and shook her head as she pulled away the clothing protectors. "Go on. You're almost done, and I can finish you up once your meeting is over."

"Great," I mumbled under my breath, and followed Meyer, Rachel, and the key production staff into the office.

Ethan closed the door, fuming. "I assume you all watched this last night, but for those of you who didn't—" He started the tape of the show on the huge television mounted on the wall. The logo appeared and the announcer stood in front of the *Cooking Masters* emblem.

"The ultrapopular cuisine show, *Cooking Masters*, has begun shooting its eighth season, and things are really starting to heat up—and not just in the kitchen. Sources say that there is more going on than just great food and competition drama. Stay tuned for more details when they become available." The announcer went on to reveal some daytime television indiscretion, and the screen went dark.

"I want to know what is going on and who in the hell is talking to these people. If we want them to have a story about this show, then we'll leak it ourselves. We have people for that."

Rachel leaned forward. "This is good for all of us. Watchers are going to wonder about the upcoming season, and the first episode hasn't even aired yet." What she said made sense to me, but there was more behind this than just some gossip on a cable TV show.

"Under normal circumstances, yes. But the network has already been hit with scandals on some of its other shows, and they won't stand for any with us. We're a pressure cooker. Let the chefs snipe and backbite at each other. That's what's supposed to happen, but as judges and producers, we're supposed to be above all this. There are rumors on the set that contestants are involved with judges and—"

"I've heard those too," I spoke up. "Don't see how that's possible, given the fact that you're supervising or filming them most of the time. The rest of us are too exhausted to worry about it. I think that's just a rumor that someone planted to stir the pot."

"We didn't have any of this trouble last season," Ethan countered, his hands on his hips.

"Then what's different?" I questioned. "You have had different chefs and guest judges before. Rachel has been on the show for five seasons. I don't know anyone to tell stories to even if I had any. Meyer wouldn't talk to gossipers. So who else is different?" I met Ethan's gaze.

"What? You want us to talk to every gaffer and soundman on the set who wasn't here before?" Ethan challenged.

"We should be doing something if this is a real concern, because yelling at us isn't going to stop the leak, and it isn't going to help put these rumors to rest. We all have just as much invested in a successful season as you do." I didn't want to sound snippy, but being taken to the woodshed for something that I had nothing to do with was not something I was going to take lying down.

Ethan trooped around the table. "What's your idea?"

I cleared my throat and glanced at Meyer and then back to Ethan. "There is more going on than just this show." I got out the messenger bag that I'd brought with me and pulled out the canary-yellow note. "I got this on Friday and thought it was a shooting change." I handed it to Ethan. "The thing is, I found another note under my plate after the desert challenge. This one was addressed to Rachel." I passed it to her. "It says nearly the same thing."

"What secret are you afraid of revealing?" Ethan asked. "I'm not a fool. I know we all have things we would like to keep private."

I purposely didn't look at Meyer. "That's just it. I don't have a secret. I think someone is fishing and trying to find something juicy. That clip you showed us didn't say anything specific. In fact, I don't think they have anything other than that juicy teaser." A picture started to form in my head. "This isn't my usual business, but is this the time of year when television shows are normally filmed?" I looked to each of the people around the table as they shook their heads.

"This is a slow time of year," Burt, the head of cinematography, explained. He looked like he had been around this business for years. "It's part of how we can get all this space. What are you getting at?"

"If it's a slow time of year for filming and production, then it's a slow time for the gossips unless some star falls off the wagon, or Justin Bieber drops his drawers on Melrose Avenue or someone else does something stupid."

They all chuckled.

"So, they need filler, and someone is supplying it to them, whether it's true or not."

Ethan nodded slowly, and Rachel smiled. "You know this town better than you think you do," she whispered to me.

"But I would suggest that if anyone does have something indiscreet going on, they tell Ethan," I explained. "He needs to know." Once again, I didn't even glance at Meyer, but those words were meant for him, and I hoped he'd take the chance. Ethan did deserve to know if Meyer and I were involved, and quite frankly, I needed to know as well. So yeah, this was a sort of test to see how serious Meyer was. It might have been very high school, but there was nothing wrong with killing two birds with one stone. "Is there anything else?" I asked Ethan.

"No," he said.

I stood. "I'm needed back in makeup and then wardrobe." I didn't say that we all had a show to tape, but I was ready to get out of there.

"Yes. We all have plenty to do, so let's get at it." Ethan dismissed everyone, and they filed out. I followed the others and returned to Darlene so she could finish.

Word got around at lightning speed about the subject of our discussion. These people gossiped faster than anyone I had ever met in my life. It seemed that Darlene knew what had happened before I even got back.

"Honey, I hear everything."

"Great. Did you hear the one about the one-legged bootlegger?" I asked.

"No," Darlene answered as she lightly applied some powder.

"Then you haven't heard everything." I shrugged, and she actually half snorted, and I let her finish her work. Once she was done, I met Rachel and Meyer, and we reviewed the challenges and the plan for the day before getting to work.

"THE SET used to be fun, but now it's nothing but pressure," I told Felix as he drove me home that evening. I was growing to like him more and more.

"That's Hollywood. No one seems to let anyone else just enjoy what's good. There's always someone who wants what you have and is willing to snatch it away."

I nodded. "Have you always lived here?"

"Yes. I was born here. I'm a true Angelino, and there are surprisingly few of us. It seems like more and more people come here every year, looking for their dream—whatever that may be."

That sounded about right to me. "What's your dream?" I asked. "Mine was to be an artist. I thought I would produce great works of art, but instead I design websites and make other people look good—well, that's how I make my living. But I used to dream of having a gallery opening and displaying my work for everyone to see." I paused and waited, hoping Felix would open up a little.

"I wanted to be a television star. As a kid, I used to watch all the shows and wondered why so few people looked like me, and when they did, they were the bad guys." He pulled to a stop at a light. "People of Latin or Spanish descent like me were always the drug dealers or the killers. But never the good guys or the leading men. That is until guys like Antonio Banderas and a few others. But even then, he ended up playing Zorro."

"But he played a lot of other characters and was in some very important movies. And his Zorro was so good, and the humor…." I smiled because I enjoyed those movies, but I did understand the point Felix was making. "I loved him in *Evita* and in *Philadelphia*— he was amazing. But I get what you're saying. Do you want to be in the movies?" I asked, and Felix shook his head.

"I want to start a movement or something so that there are more people like the rest of us on television." He seemed so earnest, and I couldn't help smiling. Such passion, especially for other people, was rare, and I got the idea that Felix was a very special man. "But that isn't a career, just a goal. I'm taking some online college courses so I can start to figure things out."

The more I talked with him, the more I realized that Felix had a good head on his shoulders.

"Do you have someone special?" I asked, and he hesitated. "You don't need to say anything if you don't want to." That was his business, and I probably shouldn't have asked.

"There is someone very special. But it's not what you think." He passed a small photo book to the back seat. "His name is Louis, and he's my son." The smiling little boy from those pictures must have been about two. The braces on his legs had me wondering what had happened to him.

"He's adorable, and that smile is precious."

"Louis is my world. Everything I do is for him." The pride and love for his son rang as clear as a bell in Felix's voice. "Right now, my mother is taking care of him while I work." Worry crept in, and I could tell there was a story there, but we made the turn off the freeway into stop-and-go traffic, and Felix grew quiet as he drove. I didn't have the right to push anyway.

Felix pulled the car up to my building, and I got out, thanking him for the ride, and went inside. Rosco greeted me at the door, and I dropped my things on the sofa and flopped down into the chair.

Rosco climbed on my lap, and I absently stroked his fur, wondering what in the hell was going on. This was supposed to be a relatively simple task: come to Hollywood, judge a cooking competition. I wasn't supposed to run into Meyer again, and all this business with the drama on set was getting ridiculous.

I absently answered my phone when it rang. "Hi, Clare," I said as brightly as I could.

"Even I can tell that was fake. What the hell is happening?" she demanded.

"Well, I love you too," I retorted.

"I know you do, and it's because I care about your picky ass, so spill," she pressed. "And don't leave out any of the good juicy stuff. Is the set a passion pit?"

"It's a cooking show. You have been watching too much tabloid television." Of course, she had seen the little story teaser. "Working on the show is longer hours and harder work than I expected it would be."

"Yeah… yeah…. What's the dirt?" she pushed. "I want the good gossip. Are the contestants sleeping with each other? Why all the secrecy and stuff?" She was like a rabid dog. "I love this kind of stuff. My life is really boring. Heck, I work for you, don't I? I need some excitement."

"And this is how you get it?" That was something I didn't understand at all.

"Sure. Why not? It doesn't hurt anyone, and it's fun. Stories about other people getting into trouble make my petty misdeeds unimportant. And I don't get to be around glamorous people all the time. You've seen the other people in the building here. It's pretty dull, and there certainly isn't California eye candy. I just want to live a little through you." She laughed, and I knew she was pretty much putting me on, though just how much was still a mystery.

"What did you really call for besides giving me grief?" I hoped she'd get to the point.

"Really… I wanted to find out how you were doing. I hinted on the blog that something really big was coming, and the comments lit up. It seems that it hasn't been leaked yet that you're a judge on *Cooking Masters*, so I thought I'd play it up as much as possible. Anyway, how are you?"

"I'm busy and tired. Rosco is doing well, though he misses you." I was stalling, trying to figure out how much to tell her. "As near as we can tell, that story on television is bullshit, but…." It was hard to deny it completely. "I will tell you this…. Meyer seems really different, and he told his parents…."

She gasped. "No fucking way? He came out of the closet? Well, that's a step in the right direction." She paused. "Wait, are you involved with him again?" She had a knife-edge in her voice.

"It's all right. I have my eyes open, and I really like this Meyer. He's caring and looks out for me the way a real boyfriend should. I haven't told anyone about us because I promised I wouldn't."

"Are you sure about this?" Boy, there was fire inside her.

"He actually asked about things between us after the show was over. I don't have any answers, but he's really different. I actually think you'd like this Meyer. He knows what he wants and is not a selfish dick. I think he's figuring it out."

Clare groaned. "Oh shit… you're falling in love with him all over again." I could see her eyes rolling. "You never got over the guy, not really…."

A knock sounded on the door.

"Is that him?" Clare demanded. "Look, you tell him that if he doesn't treat you right, I'm going to come out there and slap him to a peak and then knock the peak off. And if he hurts you, his nuts are in real danger. Tell him I'll make pâté out of them and feed it to Rosco."

Man, she was rabid. "Okay. I get the point."

"Make sure he does. Maybe the point of a knife."

Holy cow, it was wonderful to have a friend who cared about me so much.

"I'll be fine, and if he hurts me, then I'll come home and you can feed me ice cream until I pass out into a coma. We'll watch sappy movies, and I'll cry my eyes out like I did the last time." At least I knew what the awful feeling was. Heartbreak was a mistress who came around for everyone at some point. This time I'd recognize the witch.

I opened the door and let Meyer in.

"I'm going to let you go, but you'd better tell me if anything happens and I'll be on the next plane out there."

God, it was great that I had a friend like her. "I love you, and we'll talk later." I was about to hang up when she stopped me.

"You tell him what I said, because I will come for him." The cut in her voice was back, and I promised her that I would, chuckling slightly, and Meyer definitely seemed confused.

I hung up and smiled. "That was Clare." I grinned and told him what she'd said.

Meyer paled and his hands clasped in front of him. "She's scary." He shook his head, and I set the phone aside. There was no doubt that she could be damned frightening.

Meyer sat in what was becoming his place on the sofa, and I sat next to him. "I'm scared." I figured I might as well be honest about what I was thinking. "Someone is digging for some dirt, and they will do whatever they have to in order to find it." I bit my lower lip. "If someone finds out about us, what do you think is going to happen?"

Meyer shrugged. "Nothing. I had a meeting with Ethan, and I told him that you and I knew each other and had a previous relationship. I was clear that neither of us knew the other was going to be part of this season and that we have been seeing each other. I didn't go into the nature of our relationship, and when he asked, I told him it was none of his business."

To say I was shocked was an understatement. "You actually told him that you and I were in a relationship?"

"Yes. He needs to know."

It seemed so logical, and yet it was something I never thought Meyer would actually do.

"But...," I sputtered, trying to get my mind around all this. "You actually told Ethan that you're gay and that you're in a relationship with me."

Meyer scooted closer, taking my hand in his. "I told Ethan that you and I knew each other before both of us were asked to be on the show and that you and I had been friends back then."

I turned to watch him and felt Meyer's heat rising around him.

"I did tell him that you and I hadn't parted on the best of terms, but that we had worked things out between the two of us." The intensity in Meyer's eyes was enticing as all hell.

"I don't know what to say." This was the last thing I had expected to happen. "You did this to protect me... us?" My head felt cloudy for a second, and then the real meaning of what Meyer had said became clear in my mind. I narrowed my eyes and shook my head. "Wait, did you tell Ethan about us and the fact that we've been... together... or not?"

Meyer squirmed, and I pulled my hand back. "I didn't want to have someone trying to find out secrets about us. Besides, I don't think that whoever is out to dig up dirt is looking in our direction. I have no idea why, though." He patted my hand. I knew he was trying to reassure me, but it wasn't really working any longer.

I placed my hands in my lap and lowered my gaze. I didn't know why I would have thought that Meyer would have just bounded out of the closet like that. He hadn't three years ago, and while Meyer seemed to be making progress in figuring out who he was, this would have been a good chance for him to acknowledge our relationship in a controlled manner. I closed my eyes and tried not to be too disappointed. The show was becoming a pressure cooker, with everyone looking at each other, wondering who was behind this, every time a new note was delivered.

"I hope you're right." I turned to him. "But we all have secrets, and not just the ones you and I are aware of."

Meyer leaned closer. "What sort of secrets do you have? You're the last person on earth I would suspect of keeping secrets." He pressed against me, and I probably should have pulled away. Call me weak, or even dumb, but damn it all, I was falling for Meyer, and so far he had surprised me. I didn't want to let a momentary hurt undermine what might be happening between us.

I shrugged. "I'm not talking about big kinds of secrets." The kind that Meyer seemed pretty adept at managing. "But there are things I don't want spread all over the front pages of the internet. I mean, what you and I do in the bedroom is between the two of us. It isn't something I want other people knowing. Everyone deserves some privacy. Not everything is for public consumption." I sighed softly. "What about you?" I asked, and Meyer hesitated. I couldn't help wondering what he was hiding, but I didn't inquire further.

"Okay." Meyer coughed softly, clearly uncomfortable, and I could tell he was deciding if he actually wanted to tell me or not.

"All right. You don't need to come clean about what's bothering you and what you're afraid of." I was giving him an easy out and figured he'd take it. Meyer seemed to be in a retreating, secret kind of mood, and generally when that happened, it could be like he had a safe around his heart.

"It isn't that." He squirmed. "I've made some stupid decisions in my life. I can admit that, but I don't want the dumbness of those choices splashed all over everywhere." He sighed softly. "It's… look. Starting a business is really hard. There's an old saying in the restaurant business: if you want to make a small fortune, start with a large fortune and open a restaurant." He flashed a quick smile, which faded. "It's a lot more difficult than I ever thought it would be. For my first restaurant, I needed money to buy all the equipment, and no bank was going to give me that kind of a loan, so I borrowed from some people I don't recommend anyone go to for cash. I paid them back and walked away, but that isn't something I want splashed across the internet. I mean, someone could twist that, and suddenly I'm connected to the mob and my businesses are fronts for organized crime… or something." Meyer fidgeted in the seat. "At first, I thought that might have been the issue behind all this, but I doubt it. He tends to use much more… physical methods in his business. And I paid him back, in full, and had a meal delivered to him as a thank-you." Meyer wiped his forehead. "I never want to be in that kind of position again. I was lucky, *really* lucky, but things could have gone so very wrong then. And as I said, I made a stupid decision, but it worked out." He shivered, and I slid closer, putting my arm around his shoulders to comfort him.

"I wish I had known that you needed help." I would have done what I could. Hell, even after what we'd been through, I would have tried to figure out a way to get Meyer the money he'd needed. Despite the breakup and everything, I knew Meyer and food were a magical combination, and it would have been a shame to deny the world the artistry and magic that was Meyer in the kitchen.

"There was no way anyone could have helped me. A lot of chef-started restaurants have a financial backer who bankrolls the enterprise. But if I'd gone that route, then the money person would have had a lot of control over operations and eventually the food. I didn't want that. I came so close to disaster on more than one occasion, but then the business took off and I was able to get a proper loan and repay the debt."

I nodded. I could understand what he was saying. It made sense, but I figured that was some sort of cover story. Granted, Meyer didn't owe me an explanation of everything in his life any more than I owed one to him of mine.

I covered my mouth with my hand as I yawned. I tried to squelch it, but was too danged tired.

Meyer got up, went into the kitchen, and made some pasta for dinner. By the time I'd eaten, I was exhausted, and Meyer and I went to bed. I couldn't figure out anything that would be juicy about my life. I just wasn't that interesting.

I fell to sleep almost immediately and woke to the clock beside the bed glowing three minutes after two. I rolled over, staring at the ceiling, Meyer quietly sleeping next to me, with Rosco curled near my feet. At that moment, I had everything I thought I wanted. Well, I could delude myself into thinking I had it, at least.

I couldn't help wondering if things between Meyer and me weren't in the exact same place that they had been three years earlier. Damn it all, I was falling in love with Meyer once again, and the hope that he would acknowledge me and that we could have a relationship that existed in the light of day burned just as brightly as it had those years ago. And that scared the shit out of me. I had gone through hell when Meyer left, and I now was setting myself up for the exact same heartbreak all over again. History was repeating itself, and I needed to somehow get myself and my heart off this damn treadmill before I was shattered beyond repair.

I turned my head to face Meyer, his outline visible in the glow of the blinds from the lights of the city outside. Why was it that when I came close to getting what I wanted, it stayed elusive and just out of reach?

"Luke," Meyer rumbled, half-asleep. "I know you're worried, and I know I'm not helping." He rolled onto his side, and I wondered how he knew what was going through my head. "I know you, remember? I might have been stupid about how I treated you and was dumb enough to let you go, but…." He turned over to face me. "How about this? Let's get through this show without making waves so Ethan won't lose his shit, and then you and I will figure out a way forward that is open and honest for both of us." He slipped his arm around my waist, and I breathed a sigh of relief. "And yes, before you ask, you can hold me to that promise. I might not be as open about who I am with the world, but I know what I want… and who I want." He tugged me closer. "We'll figure it all out."

I closed my eyes and tried to go back to sleep, but I tossed and turned for a long while. Things with Meyer kept running through my head, as well as the situation on the set and the person looking for dirt. It pissed me off that some people couldn't be content with what they had and were determined to make a profit off the exposure of others. I also wasn't nearly as settled on the idea that whoever did this didn't have their sights set on Meyer and me. Especially with Meyer sleeping next to me, in my bed, most nights, it would be so easy to follow him here. Maybe the fact that they hadn't was a kind of proof that they weren't that interested. But who knows?

"You need to calm down, or you're going to look puffy in front of the cameras," Meyer whispered groggily, and tugged me right next to him, rolled me onto my back, and found my lips in the darkness.

"Meyer," I whispered as Rosco thumped to the floor with a soft *mrrr*, and most likely hurried out of the room.

"One way or another, you need to sleep, and this is the best way I can think of to wear you out and turn off that whirring mind of yours." He kissed me again, more forcefully, and the circular thoughts in my head settled and narrowed to Meyer, who slid down my body to worry a nipple between his lips and tongue. I gasped and thrust my chest forward, desperate for Meyer's hot, erotic attention, any way I could get it.

Meyer worked his legs between mine, his knees pushing them apart and under, guiding my legs upward. He threw off the covers, and I wound my arms around his neck. This wasn't going to be some sort of slow seduction, but a hard fucking—just what I needed. God bless him.

"That's it, babe, open yourself to me." He breathed deeply and reached to the bedside table while I inhaled his rich, sleep-intensified scent that sent my mind spinning. Dammit, if I could bottle his heady aroma, I'd never have to work again. I could call the stuff *Sex*, because that's what it was—pure, unadulterated sex in scent form. I shivered and inhaled again, wanting more as Meyer shifted.

I gasped as Meyer breached me, a digit going deep and my head spinning. He always knew how to touch me and the way to make me long for him with only the simplest touch.

"That's it," Meyer crooned, and I exhaled deep and long, relaxing the muscles as he stretched me farther.

"Oh God." My entire body undulated with desire as he pulled away. I lay still, waiting, anticipation building until Meyer pressed to my entrance, sliding inside, filling, adding heat upon fire as he slowly rocked back and forth. "Meyer... I...." He made me forget my doubts and worries. This was what I had been missing for the past three damned years.

I gasped for air as Meyer pushed deeper and held still, taking me halfway to heaven without actually doing anything. Just the fact that he was there, connected to me, was more than enough to cause my heart to race. His gaze met mine, deep and intense. I held it as he slowly undulated his hips. I moaned, releasing my hold around Meyer's neck, falling back on the bed, giving my pleasure over to him. I arched my back and moved into each thrust, going with him as Meyer pounded me halfway to oblivion. My ears rang and my head lightened as I tried to hold on to some sort of control, but Meyer ripped it away. I reached to stroke myself, becoming more and more desperate for release. Meyer batted my hand away, then stroked me in time to the undulations of his hips and the throbbing in my head.

"Meyer, God, please." I clamped my eyes closed as Meyer held me on the brink, pulling back and then bringing me to the edge once more. I reached up over my head to grab the headboard, groaning as he rammed into my body, hitting that spot each time and sending my entire body into orbit.

I was on fire, and there was no way in hell I wanted that intense heat quenched. Hanging on, it built more and more until I thought I was going to fly to pieces. Then and only then did Meyer drive harder, and I tipped over the edge into the abyss of ecstasy, flying high and long into clouds of happiness that I never wanted to return from.

When I came back down, Meyer held me. I caught my breath, and as Meyer and I separated, I quivered and gasped at the sensation. I needed some time for the tingling to subside, and yet I relished the feeling and hoped it would last. But like all good things, it came to a slow end, and I lay back down in bed with Meyer holding me. And, damn it all, I hoped everything outside my bed was all right, because right here and now, it was pretty damned special.

CHAPTER 9

"TENSION ON the set of *Cooking Masters* is thick enough to cut with a knife. Not only are the chefs heating up the show, but the judges are turning up the heat as well. Stay tuned for more." The clip cut away, and I shook my head, turning off the television.

Ethan looked around the room, and Rachel seemed on edge as well.

"It's a fishing expedition," I told Meyer and Ethan. Basically, it said no more than the last report they ran. "Someone is trying to dig up something, but they aren't having any luck." I turned to the others. "Has anyone gotten any more notes?" I asked, and Ethan paused and groaned.

"I did," he said softly, but didn't go into any details.

I glanced at Justin, who stood near the door. He seemed nervous to me. I hated my mistrust, because he had been so helpful for me here, but my suspicions seemed to be playing out. I wasn't sure how I could prove it, but Justin definitely had easy access to Ethan and his office.

"This entire situation is ridiculous, and we need to find out who is behind this and put a stop to it." Ethan quivered with anger, and his hands clenched and unclenched. "I don't know what the hell someone thinks they are doing, but this must stop, and any sort of scandal will be dealt with severely." He took a deep breath, gripping the back of the chair, glaring at everyone in the room. "If you have secrets, they had better be buried deep, and they had sure as hell better be kept away from the set." He pulled out the chair and sat down. "Let's review the day's schedule and get to work."

I glanced at Meyer and then at Rachel and the rest of the production team. Rachel sat back as though she didn't have a care in the world, but the hair on the back of my neck stood up. That was an act, and the tiny beads of perspiration on her forehead gave it away. She was worried, as were the other faces around the table. One of the techs, a man named Ryan, bit his lower lip, while another texted under the table. This was a room full of nervous people, and I couldn't blame them. Hell, I was beginning to wonder what I had in my own past that could be misconstrued and blow up in my face.

I knew that Meyer and I were playing with fire and it was a matter of time before someone figured out that things were more than friends between us. They weren't dumb, and if we were being watched, then it wasn't a huge leap of logic. As Ethan and the others talked about filming schedules and how they expected the day to unfold, I wondered just what I wanted to have happen. I had promised Meyer that I wouldn't out him, and I wasn't going to break my word. But was it bad that part of me wondered if someone might be interested in us and Meyer could get outed that way? I tried not to think about it too hard, and I certainly wasn't going to draw attention to us.

"Luke will be judging the appetizer round with Rachel, and it will be centered around broccoli. Luke, we know you hate it, so be honest and natural. We really want your reactions—"

"Be prepared for comments about battery acid and using the dish to jump-start my dying tongue." I quivered as I thought about eating cooked broccoli. *Yuck!*

"Just be honest," Ethan said with a momentary gleeful smile. "This is another challenge where we want them to make a dish you'll like."

Ethan had told me that those episodes were looking like gold to the producers, and they changed some of the later challenges because of it. Which of course meant I had to eat still more food I didn't like. Oh well, it came with the territory.

Ethan continued on, but the room was otherwise quiet, suspicion and worry hanging in the air like a thick fog.

I turned to Rachel to catch her reaction to the challenge, and she squirmed in her seat. Rachel never squirmed. She was a goddess most of the time, sitting erect in her chair, listening and taking in what she needed to do. Not today. Meyer seemed calm enough, but even Ethan paced as he talked. Each person at the table looked alternately at the others as tension ratcheted up by the second.

"Okay," I said, standing. "We need to talk about what the hell is going on. We're all getting notes and threats. Everyone is suspicious of everyone else, wondering who is up to what and what sort of secrets someone—one of us, obviously—is trying to dig up." I had had enough. "We need to concentrate on getting the best episodes we can and to hell with the rest of it." I met Ethan's gaze, and he nodded. Thank God. "This entire hotbed of worry and suspicion has to stop. Who the hell cares what someone else is doing? As long as it doesn't affect the end product, then who gives a damn? It's just fodder for people who want to know every single thing about the lives of people who happen to be on television." I stepped back and put my hands on the top of the chair. "I have a life, and I wasn't hired to spill my guts all over the place. Nor do I give the rest of America the right to know my business." I turned to each person in the room, meeting their gaze. "And let me tell you, if the person behind this is in this room and I find out who they are, I will get even."

"He will, believe me," Meyer quipped, and I rolled my eyes.

"This entire thing is a distraction. Everyone has secrets. I know I do, and I bet each of you does too. So screw it and let's get back to work." This time I centered my gaze on Ethan, who nodded and stood at the end of the table.

"I probably would have said it better, but I agree. Let's get to work." Ethan continued the meeting, and at least some of the

127

tension had been dispersed. I had little doubt that it would most likely return with the next letter, but what the hell.

"GOD, THAT was one hell of a day," Meyer said that evening in my trailer, putting his feet up across the banquette seat. "Maybe we should add a contest to see who can drop the greatest number of pans in a single day."

I chuckled. "Umm, that would be you during your demonstration." I patted him on the shoulder. "What the hell happened? You were never a butterfingers."

Meyer reached into his pocket and handed me a piece of what I was coming to dread—that damned yellow paper. "This was in my documentation. I'm not sure when it was put there or who did it." He looked down at his feet. "It says to watch the entertainment news tonight." Meyer raised his gaze and seemed pale. "I wasn't sure if I should tell you or not."

I looked over the page. "What the hell are they playing at? If they know something, then why not ask for money or something? That would be the easiest way to gain. Why go through all this shit?"

Meyer shook his head. "I don't know. But one thing I'm sure of: I've been shit wrong up until now."

A knock on the door had both of us jumping. Rosco raced up from the back bed, and I picked him up so Meyer could open the door. Rachel climbed inside, brandishing a note, pulled the door closed, then slapped it on the table.

It read the same as the one Meyer had. "What the hell do we do about this crap?" Rachel demanded.

I sighed as Rosco struggled to be let down. I set him on the floor, and he hissed and then raced for the back of the trailer like his tail was on fire. "Silly cat," I said, and motioned for Rachel to have a seat. "We need to tell Ethan." I pulled out my phone and sent him a message, giving him a brief overview of what had happened.

Within minutes he was at the door, and the small trailer was filled to capacity. "The network is having a fit about all this. They have already been on the phone with me, and I have to somehow manage this whole situation. They're worried that this innuendo is going to have a real backlash with our viewers."

"Then what do we do?" I was the novice at all this. "What *can* we do? There isn't a way to stop the story."

Ethan shook his head and then turned away, pulling aside the curtain and looking out the window in the door. "I called a friend this morning at the network to see if I could get an idea of what was going on, but they are being really tight-lipped about it. My friend did say that they had something juicy on people involved with the show and that they were going to run with it in a big way."

My hand began to tingle, and I turned to Meyer and then to Rachel. I could tell Meyer was as nervous and jittery as a skydiver with a ripped parachute. It was hard for me to read Rachel, but she seemed upset as well.

"I suggest we all come to the production office. We need to watch this damned show so we know what we're dealing with, and then we can figure out a way to deal with the fallout." Ethan's suggestion seemed logical, and we all agreed.

I called Felix to let him know about the change in plans for the evening. Rachel and Ethan trudged out of the trailer, and Meyer grew even more nervous.

"What is the worst that could happen?" I asked once the door was closed.

"That's easy for you to ask. Everyone knows about you. But if me being gay comes out in an ugly way, it could affect more than the show. It could affect my business and the way I make my living. It's possible that I would never get any more television work, and…." He hung his head. "What if people stay away and don't want to eat in my restaurants any longer? Look at Paula Deen, for God's sake. Yeah, she did some stupid things about hiring at her restaurant, but they happened years ago, and for a long time, no one would touch her with a ten-foot pole. I don't want that." He put his hands over his face, then held his head. "You know, this is my fault. Hiding didn't do me any good."

"We all have to learn that we can't hide from ourselves. I think that's a big part of being gay. Learning to accept that part of yourself that might not fit in with everyone else." I slid onto the bench across from him, my hands folded together on the table.

"I keep hoping that the story isn't about you and me," Meyer said. "I only wanted to get through this show, and then I could come out on my own terms and manage the process."

"I wish that too." But I was afraid that choice was going to be taken away from him, and it made me angry. Yes, Meyer had hurt me because of his decision to stay in the closet. But there was more to it. Love and relationships were always a two-way street, and there were other problems, *my* problems. I had needed to be more forceful and stand up for myself and what I wanted. Meyer and I hadn't done a good job of communicating with each other. We needed to talk more and not just let our bodies do the speaking for us in bed. "Do you have a publicist?" I asked, speaking off the top of my head.

"No. I haven't needed one until now."

"Then you'll get one," I told him. "Tomorrow. Whatever happens, we'll let a professional handle it. They can manage the press and help us build positive stories. This isn't going to be the end of the world, even though it might feel like it right now." Fear really sucked.

Meyer took a deep breath and checked his watch. "We might as well go over and see how bad this is going to be."

I was about to slip out of the seat when Rosco trotted up, jumped into Meyer's lap, and rubbed against his chest.

"You know, your cat might be fickle." Meyer rubbed down Rosco's back. "I thought he hated me."

"He knows who he likes, and anyway, I have a theory. Cats and dogs have great senses of smell. Maybe when we hide and lie about things, they can smell it. Rosco has always been a pretty good judge of character." I stood and lifted Rosco onto the floor. He immediately jumped back onto Meyer's lap, rubbing against him again. "Stubborn cat." I lifted Rosco off again and carried him to the back bed. He immediately jumped down, ran to the door, and plopped himself right in front of it, glaring at me.

"Take him along. He's sort of the shoot mascot, and after this bloodbath, some comfort might be nice." Meyer shook as he got to his feet.

I scooped Rosco up, opened the door, and carried him outside. "Here are the keys," I told Meyer, and he locked the trailer. Then the three of us traipsed across the lot to the production office. We all sat quietly around the table in the conference room, with the television muted. It felt like we were at a funeral.

Rosco jumped down as soon as I sat, pouncing into Meyer's lap and settling down.

"You had to bring that cat," Rachel snapped, and I wondered just where her gentle persona had gone. Maybe it was the pressure, but this situation certainly hadn't brought out Rachel's best qualities.

Justin came in and spoke to Ethan quietly. Ethan got up without saying a word and stalked out of the room. The rest of us were left to stew and wonder what was next. He returned just before the show was set to air. He plopped into his seat, swiveling it toward the large television screen. I shifted my chair closer to Meyer's and waited as the show logo emblazoned the room.

Damn, it was frustrating waiting through story after story, teaser after teaser with no substance. The show was nearly over, and I was starting to think the notes were another ruse when a logo flashing *EXTRA* filled the screen.

"We have a late-breaking story. Many of you have no doubt been wondering what is up with the amazing cooking-contest drama *Cooking Masters*. Well, we have an exclusive from a source within the show itself, and you're going to want to stay tuned. We'll give you all the news right after this break."

I checked my watch and groaned. Apparently they were going to make a big deal of whatever it was, because the show only had five minutes to go, and that meant they were going to play this up to the hilt. But first the ads for bleach and laundry soap, which were probably appropriate for a show like this—after watching it, you needed to wash and bleach your brain from all the inanity. Still, I could understand how people got hooked. The show was designed to entice and dangle juicy carrots in front of the viewer.

"We're back, and we have the scoop," the perky announcer said, setting my teeth on edge. "*Cooking Masters* is well into the taping of its eighth season, and it seems there has been heat in the kitchen that isn't coming from the stoves."

I rolled my eyes at the bad copy, but kept my gaze glued to the screen.

"It seems that Emmy-nominated host and judge Rachel Graham has been taking some liberties. Reports say that Ms. Graham and a contestant from season seven had had an affair before and while season seven was being taped. Officials of the long-running cooking contest, which has made just about everyone in America run to their kitchen to recreate the amazing dishes, have said that the indiscretion of one of their hosts in no way affected the outcome of the show, since the contestant in question was kicked off halfway through that season."

The announcer paused, and it was all I could do not to breathe a visible sigh of relief and high-five Meyer, who sat next to me. Instead, I hazarded a glance at Rachel, who stared aghast at the screen. And when she noticed I was watching, she schooled her expression to one of haughty derision.

"No one is going to buy that load of crap!" Rachel shouted as the announcer continued. "How in the hell could anyone have an affair with one of our contestants when we're watching them almost all the damned time?"

No one answered her charge.

"We're all wondering how this will affect Ms. Graham's contract with the show, which we understand is up after this season. Stay tuned, and we'll keep you updated on all the late-breaking entertainment news. Good night, and good watching!"

The ending credits began to run, and I pushed my chair back, with Rosco jumping in my lap.

I was stunned, sitting in the chair without moving. The entire room was suddenly made of glass, and the first comment was going to shatter everything. But then it occurred to me that it had already been broken. If Rachel's contract was indeed up after this season, maybe the producers had decided not to renew. The thing was, they certainly were unlikely to renew it now, with that kind of scandal. A judge and a contestant… no way. That kind of rumor was enough to kill a career.

"That's enough of that, everyone," Ethan finally said, and I glanced at Justin, wondering again what he had to do with this. "Go home. We have an episode to film in the next two days, and we're not going to get behind now."

He stalked out of the room without another word, and I took the chance to escape as well, with Rosco in my arms. Meyer followed, as did most of the others. A few of the people in Rachel's inner circle stayed behind, but I had little doubt that her sphere of admirers had just taken a huge numbers hit, and the rest were certain to follow.

I called Felix to tell him I was ready to go home. The way I figured it, Meyer and I had gotten a reprieve from discovery and revelation, and it was now up to him how he wanted to handle it.

"Luke," Meyer called as he half jogged down the stairs of the production office.

"Gentlemen," Ethan said as he approached from around the corner. "I would like a word with both of you in the morning. There are a number of things that we will need to discuss about the future—your futures. I'll see you at my office at eight." He smiled, and a car pulled up. Ethan got inside, waved, then closed the door, and the black car glided away.

"What do you think that's about?" Meyer asked.

"If I had to guess, I'd say it's to review the terms of our parole...."

Felix pulled to a stop, and I set Rosco inside the car and began to get in myself.

"Do you want to get dinner?" Meyer asked.

I paused, because I really wanted to see him, but it was taking a chance. "You're a chef. Is there a place that can cook better than you?" I climbed into the car, and Felix pulled away.

"I watched the show," Felix said. "Who would have thought she'd make that kind of mistake."

I coughed and cleared my throat. "What does that mean?"

Felix pulled to a stop at a light. "Rachel Graham is a barracuda, no question. She has a reputation for being kind and gentle, but in real life, there are plenty of bodies that she's stepped over to get where she is. They keep quiet mostly out of fear." Felix pulled through the intersection.

"I had no idea. She seemed nice to me," I commented.

Felix hummed softly. "That's probably because she either didn't see you as a threat or she wanted you lulled into a false sense of security. At least that's what I heard."

"Huh," I said quietly, trying to figure all of this out but not really getting anywhere. Had whoever had been stirring up trouble been after Rachel all along in order to get even? If so, then why send notes to everyone else? I still didn't have all the answers, but I was relieved that the attention seemed to be focused elsewhere for a while. "Would you tell me anything else that you know? There seems to be an entire undercurrent that I was completely oblivious to."

Felix laughed as he continued driving, then once again pulled to a stop, this time hard enough that Rosco protested softly. I hoped he didn't get carsick. That would be pretty bad. I picked up Rosco off the floor and held him, stroking his fur, comforting Rosco as he calmed me. I'd had no idea that agreeing to judge a cooking show would lead to so much drama.

I sat back in the seat, figuring I had probably gotten as much information from Felix as I could. Not that I fancied myself a detective or anything, but I wasn't getting very far. Sherlock Holmes I definitely wasn't. But I was curious, and the more I learned, the more I wondered just how many undercurrents ran through the team that made up our little piece of television.

I pulled out my phone and messaged Meyer. *What's the plan?* The more I thought about it, the more I thought getting together wasn't the best idea.

At grocery store. Will be over when I'm done. I think we need to talk and try to figure things out, Meyer sent in return.

Do you think that's a good idea? What if— I paused, not sure how to say what I wanted to. I wanted Meyer to come over because I didn't want to spend the entire night wondering about what was going to happen, but being together could add fuel to the fire and give our little note sender more stories to peddle.

Before I could send my text, a second message came through from Meyer.

Don't know if it's a good idea to get together, but I need to see you, Meyer sent, and my resolve melted.

I deleted my unfinished text and sent that we should be back at the apartment in ten minutes or so. I set my phone on the seat next to me with a sigh, returning my attention to Rosco. I actually started to talk to him, but stopped myself because I didn't want Felix to think I had gone crazy, talking to my cat like one of those lonely people with no one else to hear their voices.

"How are things going with you?" I asked Felix.

He shrugged. "The same as always."

"How's Louis?" I asked, and saw Felix smile in the mirror. Instantly, the air in the car seemed to warm and glow with excitement.

"He's great. Mom sent me a picture today." Felix passed his phone back, and I glanced at the picture of Louis in his leg braces, standing out in front of a small house. "She said he took a few steps on his own." Damn, Felix's voice broke a little. "They told us he might never be able to, but he's proving them all wrong. Louis is a determined little boy."

"That's so wonderful." I handed the phone back. "What kinds of things does he like?"

"Trucks and cars. He makes engine noises all the time and scoots around on the floor with them in his hands. Mama says I need to get him developmental toys, whatever those are."

"Play-Doh," I offered. "Things he can make stuff with. Sounds to me like Louis is really smart."

Felix nodded as he pulled the car to a stop at the intersection right near the apartment. "He really is. I just want him to be happy."

"I know you do." I wanted to pat him on the shoulder, but kept my hands to myself as he made the final turn and pulled up to the building. I carried Rosco out and arranged for Felix to pick me up in the morning, then went inside.

In the apartment, Rosco made a beeline for his food dish as soon as I set him down, probably making sure the pieces of his food that he had been saving were still there. He trotted back, giving me his "Where's my dinner?" look, and then waited while I fed him. He was getting as queeny as the boys in a West Hollywood drag show.

Meyer came in as I was washing the makeup off my face, and he got himself set up in the kitchen. It was small and there wasn't much room for a second person, but he and I made do and had a lot of fun. He wanted me to stir the sauce, so I reached around him and my hands got a little busy. While I nearly burned part of dinner, the heat in the kitchen, under my palms as they slid up beneath Meyer's shirt, was more than satisfying.

"Here," Meyer whispered, his voice low and rough. He placed his hands on mine, and we moved together. It was a strange dance to the beat of the stove and food, but I liked it. I had forgotten how much fun it could be to cook with him.

"Do you want to slice the bread for me?" he asked, and got me a place set up. Then he guided me away from the stove, and I got to work. Of course, Meyer had to check what I was doing—to supervise—and he preferred a very close supervision, with him pressed to my back.

"Meyer, this is a lot of fun, but we need to talk." Damn, I hated to break the playful mood, but things were getting serious.

"I know." He tested what he had on the stove and made some adjustments, then let me taste. "It's a simple sauce for the pork."

I closed my eyes. "Oh, that's good." It would be so easy to imagine the two of us like this, and I was trying to keep some sort of distance, to stop myself from falling that last short way. I was failing miserably and knew it.

"I'm not dumb, Luke. I know after everything that this is a bad idea. I should just go home and stay there, keep to myself, and wait for the season to be over. Then I could call you and maybe we could see each other. But by then you would be home in Philadelphia, and I'd be here, chewing the inside of my lip and wondering—again—if things couldn't have been different." Meyer turned down the burners and set the spoon in the sink. "I love food—you know that. It's my passion and what I want to build my life around. At least that's what I told myself when I left." He leaned back against the counter with a soft sigh. "I told myself then that I could be a success and make some of the best food anywhere. If I did that, then I could be happy. And guess what?" He swallowed.

"I don't know, Meyer. Since you never called, I'm going to guess that you were happy." Okay. A little pissiness came forward.

"Luke, I didn't call because I would have come back. I couldn't have stayed out here and done what I needed to do if I had done that." The ache in Meyer's voice was almost too much for me to take. That couldn't be faked. "Like I said, I thought the food would be enough. It wasn't, and I knew that as soon as I saw you again. The restaurants and the food, the fame—none of it will be enough once you go back home and I'm alone again." He swallowed and pushed away from the counter, moving closer, but I put out my hands, closing myself off.

"I need for you to say what it is you have to." I wanted to hear it, and I think Meyer needed to say it.

"It's pretty simple. I could have stayed home, but I didn't want to. See, I know now… I understand. I want you more than I want the food and the fame. I want this—us—more than all the rest of it. I couldn't have stayed home tonight any more than I could stop breathing or not eat a perfectly made soufflé." He gasped, his chest rising and falling quickly, and I swallowed around the lump in my throat. "See, Luke, I want you more than the food—more than anything."

I lowered my arms, and Meyer came to me, holding me tightly, clutching me, his fingers entwining in my hair, making my head tingle, and I held him in return. I needed Meyer, and I could admit it now.

"I need to be here with you."

I sniffed and buried my face in Meyer's shoulder. "What do we do now?"

"I don't know. But you and I will figure it out. Whatever comes, I'm not going to give you up. So if I have to rent a billboard to say that you're mine, then I will. I can't hide any longer, and if someone wants to follow me here and hide in the bushes to get something salacious, then let them. I can't fight this, and I don't want to."

"So you're willing to pay the price? Because there will be one, you know that. Someone isn't going to like that we're together, and some people might stay away from the restaurants. Who knows?"

"Yes, I know. But there's only one person I don't want staying away, and that's you." He clutched me so tightly that I could barely breathe, and yet I'd stay just like that forever. "If people don't like that I'm gay, so be it. I can't change any of that, and I don't want to hide any longer. I'd like to finish out this season on the show so you and I don't become a distraction, but what the hell. If it happens, it happens." Meyer backed away, turning to the stove.

"What is it?" His demeanor and stance had changed.

"I didn't know it would feel like this. I hadn't known what it would be like when I decided I'd had enough and it was time to just come clean, as it were. I was expecting something grand and momentous…. Instead, it's a relief. I know what I want and I can have it."

I placed my hand in the center of Meyer's back, just to have contact with him. "Yes. There is something pretty special when you figure out that you aren't going to fight yourself any longer." I inhaled and drew closer. "That dinner smells amazing. I'm going to set the table, and then after we eat your meal, I'll serve up the dessert… on sheets." I wagged my eyebrows and left the room, because if I didn't, I wasn't going to be able to keep my hands to myself and it was likely I would jump the man while he was still cooking.

Setting the table was difficult with Rosco deciding he wanted to help me. I nudged him away from the table multiple times until he finally got bored and went to explore his dish, which seemed to have sprouted something interesting, thanks to Meyer.

"I try to keep my guys happy."

I liked being one of his guys.

I finished with the table as Rosco ambled away from his dish, most likely to take a nap. God, what would it be like to have a cat's life?

"Dinner will be about fifteen minutes. Why don't you go shower if you want, and by the time you're done, I'll be ready."

I wasn't going to argue. I went to the bathroom and started the water before stripping down. Desire and arousal had simmered right on the edge for long enough that as soon as the hot water coursed over me, it threatened to break free. Taking myself in hand would be so easy, and relief begged, but I held firm, washed quickly, and then got out and dressed.

Damn, was I glad I had waited once I stepped out of the bedroom and into the dining area. Candles glowed on the table, and Meyer brought plates from the kitchen and set them at our places.

"Wow, you've never done this before."

"Nope. Not for you or anyone. I've served important and romantic dinners to plenty of couples, but I never did one for you. I thought it was time that changed." He reached for the bottle of wine, pulled the cork, and poured us each a glass, then motioned to a chair as he returned to the kitchen and brought back the warmed bread and herbed butter with him. "I tried to make what I remembered were some of your favorites. A little pasta with a light sauce, some pork with a pan sauce that made your eyes close, and of course a few lovely vegetables in a little butter with some herbs and onion. You always had simple taste in food."

"And complicated taste in men," I clarified. "We can't all like everything."

"Nope." He sat down and lifted his glass. "How is your blog? I read it sometimes. It always makes me smile. You talk about what you don't like, but you do it with such humor."

I took a bite of the pork and hummed. It was well seasoned, with a hint of heat that made my tongue tingle. It was pretty awesome. "I really try to talk about my food issues and make fun of myself a little for having them. It's disarming, and I hope it helps my readers." I took another bite and then a sip of the wine. This was an amazing meal, and instantly I was famished—in more ways than one.

"SWEETHEART," MEYER said.

I lifted my head off the pillow, a pleasant soreness reminding me of Meyer's efforts the night before. "What?" I groaned, and buried my face back in the pillow. "It isn't even light out." God, I did not want to get up. Between the bottle of wine that Meyer and I drank at dinner and the intensely athletic lovemaking, I had been wrung out and had no more to give. Sleep was needed, and my body still craved it, almost as much as it did the immensely caring and studly hot man next to me.

"We have to get up and meet Ethan."

I groaned and pushed back the covers. "How can you be so chipper?" I trudged toward the bathroom, nearly walking into the wall.

"I didn't sleep much, so I figured I might as well get up. I'll have a light breakfast for you once you're awake."

I cracked my eyes open, managing to make it into the bathroom this time, sitting down to take care of business, and holding my head. I kept wondering why I felt like a kid being called to the principal's office. But that's what this morning resembled. I finished and cleaned up, dressed in clothes that would be easy to change out of once I got to wardrobe, and met Meyer for a light breakfast.

"Why aren't there any carbs? I would kill for a bagel," I grumped as I sat down and ate the half grapefruit that Meyer had set out for me.

"Someone's being a pain in the tuckus this morning," Meyer said as he sat down across from me. "I don't remember you being a real morning-hating kind of person."

"I'm not. It's just that I'm worrying about what Ethan wants. His 'invitation' sounded pretty ominous." I finished eating and set down my spoon and napkin. "Maybe I'm blowing this out of proportion."

"Remember what we said last night. Whatever it is, we will figure it out together." Meyer seemed so calm, and I wondered why I was getting jittery and realized it was for him. I didn't want him hurt or pressured into doing something he might not be ready for. Yes, I wanted him to be able to live his life honestly, but I believed it should be on his terms and in his time, not someone else's.

"We'd better go." I stood. "Rosco, are you going to come?" He'd been nowhere to be found and still didn't make an appearance. I went into the bedroom and found him curled up near my pillow, the little scamp. I lifted him and carried him out of the apartment, and we went down. Meyer said goodbye and went to his own car, while I met Felix for my ride into the studio. The arrangements seemed stupid but necessary, or at least they had been up until now.

Rosco got comfortable, and I tried to relax but remained on edge as Felix navigated morning rush hour and pulled through the studio gates and up to the production office. I thanked him and took Rosco to the trailer, checking that he had food and water, then trudged back to the production office and went inside.

Ethan was waiting, and I sat in his office until Meyer arrived a few minutes later. Ethan closed the door and walked behind his desk. "All right. I don't know who you two think you're fooling, but I'm not one of them. You dodged a bullet yesterday, and you need to fix it." He stood with his hands on the back of his chair.

I glanced at Meyer, who had gone pale. "Ethan… I…." The words refused to come.

He shook his head and pulled out the chair. "I've been around the block more than once, and I know when two people are falling in love. I've seen it more times than I can count. Like I said yesterday, I made a call to a contact at the network and found out what story they were running. I couldn't get them to pull it, but I did give them one that they thought was much juicier and with a lot more meat on it."

My mouth hung open. "You told them about Rachel?"

"I helped confirm it for them, yes. There have been rumors, and the two of them have been seen together since taping ended last season." He leaned forward. "The producers have been on the edge about whether to renew her contract or not, and then they started seeing your tape and how much the contestants reacted to you." Ethan looked right at me. "You're fair with each of them; you

142

often have a kind word, even when you say something awful about their food, including not feeding it to your cat, which was totally brilliant and honest. There isn't much honesty in this business, but you have it, and we believe viewers are going to respond to it."

I sat back but gripped the arm of the chair. "They want to replace Rachel with me?"

"Yes. But…." His expression softened. "Actually, they're leaning toward both of you for next year. So you need to figure out how you are going to deal with what's between you. If this is some itch that needed to be scratched and you've done that, then go your separate ways and have it be over with. But if it's more than that… then make it honest. We can market you as a couple, and that will come across to viewers. But you need to shit or get off the pot."

I thought Meyer was going to swallow his head, the way he gasped, "You're serious?"

"It's okay. I think we can speak freely here." I turned to Meyer. "We'll do whatever you want to do. There's no pressure." I took his hands and held them. It was strange and wonderful to do that in front of someone else. "I get the feeling you were prepared to take on the world."

"At least most of Hollywood," Meyer quipped, and I rolled my eyes.

"Rachel's contract isn't going to be renewed," Ethan reiterated. "The producers have made that perfectly clear. I'm not sure who this letter writer is, but whoever is behind these notes and this campaign to dig up some dirt, they might have done the two of you a favor."

"No. They were after us," I told Ethan with a sigh.

"I think they were after whatever story they could sell, and they got a whiff of something between you and sold the story to the network. I wasn't able to get any information about who is behind this, so they're still out there. And the story about the two of you isn't going away. It's just been overshadowed for the moment. So, like I said, you need to figure out how you want to handle it.

The production company will have no comment either way, and of course a final decision on the next season won't be made until after this season is over." Ethan paused dramatically and leaned over the desk. "How you handle this will determine what happens."

I didn't know what to say. This was up to Meyer more than me. I knew what I wanted, but I wasn't sure how he wanted to proceed.

"You have to make a decision quickly."

I clutched Meyer's hand, hoping he didn't pull away. I turned to Ethan with determination. "You want Meyer to make a choice about how he wants to go public about something that's very personal. Who he loves is no one else's business." Anger grew in my gut. This wasn't fair at all.

"What I want doesn't matter. The news runs at a mile a minute here, and it's hard to stay in front of a story. But we have a chance to do just that here." Ethan sat back in his chair. "It doesn't have to be a big thing, and we aren't going to hire a brass band. But we can set up an interview on one of the morning talk shows. That's usually a gentler and more sympathetic interview in front of a responsive audience. If that's what you want, I'll have someone arrange it. Let me know by eight tomorrow morning what you want to do, and I'll get things in motion." That was clearly a dismissal, and we all stood. "I'll understand and support whatever you decide."

Meyer and I left the office and went to wardrobe, where I was given the clothes to wear for the day and bumped into Justin on the way out.

"How are things going?" he asked. "You really seem to be working out."

"I'd like to think so." I tried to be as normal and casual as I could, but I wanted to keep my distance. Which made me sad, because Justin had been my first friend. I hated suspicion—it cast a long black shadow, and I knew most of the time it was over innocent people. But I didn't know what else to do. "I'm only here for a few more weeks, though, and then I'll go home to my life and figure things out from there." I was keeping my answers as bland as I could. "What about you?"

Justin shrugged. "After this, hopefully Ethan will want to keep me on for his next project, but you never know." He really seemed worried, and maybe that was what was motivating him to try to make some extra money. I had to mentally pause my thinking because I didn't know for sure if Justin was behind this or not. I was learning just how easy it was to jump to conclusions.

"I hope so too," I told him. "I really need to get to makeup before they shove me in front of the cameras looking as boring as I really am." I flashed a smile and hurried off. I didn't like that I felt like I had to run away from a friend. This whole thing sucked, and I wanted it to end. The edginess was getting to be a little much.

"DAMN, YOU were funny," Meyer said as soon as we ended taping for the day.

"I was just honest. I told them up front that I tend to like broccoli when it's used raw in a dish, yet most of them cooked the danged stuff. And one of the chefs who didn't cook it put the damned thing on the plate in huge chunks." I shivered. "The best one was that tangy salad, and the worst was the one that tasted like he'd dunked the stuff in the battery of his car." I hadn't been able to keep quiet about that one. "I swear he had gone all out to make a dish that I would find inedible."

Meyer chuckled and shook his head. "I think a lot of them find it a kind of dare to actually see if they can make something that will surprise you. They're chefs and they like a challenge. I have to give you credit, you tried each dish and didn't shy away."

"God, I wanted to. The very idea of eating some of those dishes was almost more than I could stand." Thankfully I only had to eat a bite of each one, and I was getting better at it. That didn't mean I necessarily liked the food, but I was able to eat it and be glad I didn't have to have more. I supposed that was progress.

We left the studio as the chefs spent some time talking among themselves in the "stew" room. It wasn't a challenge where someone was eliminated, so my quips and comments hadn't had a great effect on the outcome of the overall contest, other than giving the winner an advantage. Still, there was plenty going on—it just didn't involve Meyer and me. I was happy to have been dismissed for the day.

"I need to get Rosco," I told him. "Then maybe we can meet for dinner." I stepped a little closer and lowered my voice. "I don't want to talk here." I slowed to add a little more distance between us. "I'll see you later."

I went to my trailer and glanced around, inhaling and squinching up my nose. Something smelled awful, sickly chemically, like maybe gas. I unlocked the door, throwing it open, only concerned for Rosco. It was hot as hell inside, and when Rosco barreled out, I caught him before he could get away. The floor was wet with moisture from the refrigerator. I held Rosco and walked around the side. The power cord had been unplugged, and the scent, which I recognized now as propane, was even stronger. I went around the front, turning off both tanks, and the scent quickly dissipated. Then I called Ethan and asked him to get studio security.

Men in blue uniforms hurried up. I wasn't sure how effective they would be, but their professionalism surprised me. I told them what I'd found and that I'd shut off the gas. "I didn't want anyone to get hurt."

"Did you see anyone?" the guard asked as he placed his hand on the outside of the tanks. "The one is empty, and the other is nearly so."

I shook my head. "No. I only smelled it and got Rosco out." He was getting fussy, and I asked one of the guards to get the carrier, bowls, and litter box from inside. I told him where they were, and he came out with them in his hands.

"We'll need to get someone to clean up in there. It doesn't look like anyone got in, but the refrigerator is a mess, and I don't want to open it."

I wasn't particularly keen on it either.

"I'll take care of it," Justin offered. I hadn't realized he had joined us, and there wasn't a way I could logically say no. This entire situation had me on edge.

"Thanks," I told him, and got Rosco in the carrier. After answering some questions, I called Felix, and he picked me up along with all the cat supplies.

Meyer had driven himself, and he sent a text asking me to meet at his place. I told Felix the address, and he took me to a small house in one of the northern suburbs. It was nice, with mature shrubs and landscaping. It had probably cost a fortune, and I wondered if Meyer had bought or was only renting it. I rang the bell, and Meyer answered the door, welcoming me inside.

The house was gorgeous and comfortable, with overstuffed furniture in a craftsman style that just begged to be sat on. The tables were honey oak, and the lamps were leaded glass and cast a warm glow. "Wow," I whispered, and set Rosco down along with the dishes. He explored the room, checking every inch while I turned to Meyer. "What's the plan?"

"I don't know. I don't want to do a stupid interview and talk about things between you and me. We get to spend only so much time together, and I want that to be just between the two of us. But if we have to do this, then…."

I put the litter box in the bathroom and sat down on the sofa, and Meyer sat next to me. "We don't have to do anything that you don't want to. This isn't about me, but you. Everyone already knows I'm gay, and there has been nothing said about it as far as I know. This is about you and what you need." I wrapped my arms around his waist and put my head against his chest. "What is it you want?"

"I just want to have you and figure things out after this is over. I want to go to bed next to you and wake up in the morning with you, and then we can determine how to build a life. I wasted three years, and I don't want to be apart any longer."

"But where? My home is on the other side of the country, and...."

Meyer put his arms around my shoulders. "I know you work from home, and you can write and manage your blog from anywhere you are." He released me, and I pulled away as Meyer stood and took my hand. He guided me out of the room and opened a door just inside the hall. "I set this up as an office, but I never use it, and I thought you could." He motioned, and I stepped inside perfection. A beautiful oak table served as a work surface, with shelves and a chair across from the desk. An actual visitor's chair.

"You want this to be for me?"

"Yes. And there's more." We continued down the hall, and he opened another door. This room contained a king-size bed with a grand, thick duvet that beckoned me forward. "This is really lonely without you."

"So you're asking me to come here and live with you... here?"

"Yes. You and I will finish the season, and then if you agree, you'll move here—in here, in this house—with me." He swallowed, and I marveled, since I'd never expected to actually hear that offer from Meyer. It was a little overwhelming. "You don't need to give me an answer right now, but think about it."

I shook my head, staring at the bed and everything it represented. "How can you just do this? You're going from closet to out and proud in what seems like seconds. It seems like too much all at once."

"I thought you'd be happy," Meyer said, confused and touched with fear.

"No, I am. And I'm so thrilled for you, and you've made me so very happy. But what about all this with the show and Ethan?

We dodged a bullet today, and you're acting like it's nothing. I'm happy with my life and I know who I am. You're the one I'm worried about. What are you going to do when the rubber hits the road and things get hard?"

Meyer took a deep breath and released it slowly. "That depends on whether you're going to be here with me or not." He sat down in the chair. "I'll send a message to Ethan and tell him that I'll do an interview if he can arrange it."

"*We'll* do an interview," I corrected. "I'll be there with you. That is, if you're serious about things being you and me?" My gaze was a challenge, but this was a test. And from the smile on Meyer's lips, I knew he'd passed.

"Okay. Together." Meyer pulled out his phone and sent a message. "Ethan said he'll arrange it tonight and give us the details tomorrow." His phone chimed again. "He also said to say nothing to anyone." Meyer set down his phone, and I wondered if he was going to collapse right there. This was all becoming very real. "I'm going to have to talk about my feelings and answer questions about my sexuality. Do you know how uncomfortable that is?"

"Yes, I do. But rather than talk about that, just concentrate the talk about us. Tell them how you left and then found me again. Make *us* the story instead of only you. That way we're together and you aren't standing alone." It was all I could come up with. "And if there's a question that's too prying, I'll jump in and try to say something cute. Let them laugh with me rather than get to the nitty-gritty details." I squeezed his hand and then hugged him. "I'm so proud of you for doing this. It almost makes the last three years worth it, just to be with you, happy, whole, and honest with yourself."

Meyer held me tighter. "I'm scared to death."

"Yeah, but we'll do it together." I kept reiterating that to him because I didn't want Meyer to feel alone for a second. There was a point in every life, at least I thought so, when you felt you were utterly alone, and this was one of those moments. You realized that you were different from most people and that differences weren't always celebrated. It was so easy to pull back into yourself. I had thought about it more times than I could count, but being out and proud of who you were was more rewarding in the long run. I only hoped this proved to be that for Meyer.

CHAPTER 10

WHEN ETHAN put his mind and will behind something, he made it happen, that was for sure. Late the following morning, Felix drove Meyer and me to a taping of one of the afternoon talk shows. Because of the time difference, it was actually taped in the morning to be run a few hours later.

"You didn't sleep at all last night," I observed, and Meyer nodded. "You need to relax and just be yourself." Like I should be talking. I had even less experience in front of the cameras than he did, and none whatsoever with this sort of situation. All I could really do was be there for him.

"I'll be okay." He turned to me and smiled. It was forced, but he was trying to make an effort for my sake.

"You don't have to do this. I know it's what Ethan wants, because it makes his life easier and he doesn't have to explain things to anyone. But it's what you want that really counts."

Meyer sighed and hugged me to him. "That's what I love about you. To hell with everyone else and what they think. I swear you'd travel to the ends of the earth if it would make me happy. I know that, and maybe it's time for me to make that same commitment." He held me a little tighter. "This is the right thing to do."

"About ten minutes," Felix said.

I settled next to Meyer, trying to soothe his nerves. Thankfully they seemed to disappear as soon as we reached the studio and were escorted inside and to the green room by an assistant.

Marla Waters was an amazing television host, and she had her audience in the palm of her hand. She wasn't a shock-and-awe interviewer and didn't do dysfunctional family dramas or "Who's the daddy?" shows. She was honest, and that came through to her audience. She could tug at heartstrings better than anyone else on television, so to be sitting in her green room was a surprise and a kind of dream come true.

"Marla is preparing for the show," an assistant said, "but she'll be in before taping." He looked both of us over. "You're dressed perfectly, so I just need to get you set up for a little makeup and we'll be ready." He sat down across from us. "There is nothing to be nervous about." He smiled brightly.

"Thanks," I said, and we followed him to makeup stations. It was surprising how quickly I'd gotten used to this process. Once they were done, we sat and waited, then talked to Marla briefly when she stopped in, until we were called to the stage. The lights went down, and the entire space seemed to glow with excitement and energy.

"Thank you all!" Marla said as the applause died down. "We have a special show for you today. Two of the judges from the upcoming season of *Cooking Masters* are here with us today. It's my pleasure to introduce acclaimed chef Meyer Thibodeau and the fabulously funny blogger of *The Pickiest Eater in America*, Luke Walker."

The audience applauded as we walked on stage. As soon as the lights hit us, I understood what it felt like to be on total display and, dang, I had to stop myself from turning around and running away. It was frightening.

"Welcome, gentlemen," Marla said, shaking hands with both of us and offering us chairs. "How is the new season of *Cooking Masters* progressing? I know I'm looking forward to it." She leaned closer. "Can you tell us who's in the lead?"

Meyer leaned nearer to her as though he was going to share a secret. "My lips are sealed."

"And so are mine. But seeing you in person, it's definitely tempting," I added, and she smiled as she turned back to the audience.

Meyer winked, and Marla laughed. "This season is going to be the best one yet. We have talented chefs and great challenges for them." Meyer turned forward toward the camera. "But there have been a number of challenges that aren't all in the kitchen."

Marla nodded slowly. "Yes. I understand there has been some drama surrounding this season."

Meyer cleared his throat, and I had to stop myself from reaching over to take his hand. I could feel his nerves and wanted to comfort him. "Yes, there has, and, well... things have gotten a little out of hand in that department." Meyer sat back, trying to get comfortable, but that wasn't happening in these stage chairs, which must have been designed to ensure that no guest wanted to sit in them for an entire show. "You see, Luke and I knew each other before I left Philadelphia for Los Angeles. That was, what...?"

"About three years ago," I supplied.

"Yes. And I never forgot him. I wasn't consulted, but there he was, and Luke and I were working together." Meyer held his breath and grew quiet.

"Did something happen between you?" Marla asked, but Meyer swallowed hard.

"Yes. We snarked at each other like there was no tomorrow," I answered, and the audience snickered softly. "I picked on him like crazy, teased, and was generally nasty."

"I deserved it," Meyer clarified with a smile. "See, I left him." Meyer turned to me, and in that brief moment, lost in Meyer's gaze, the audience disappeared. "Luke and I were lovers back in Philadelphia, and I was too afraid back then of who I was to accept myself and what I had." Meyer's voice broke a little, but he seemed to recover. "When I got the chance, I left, and we hadn't seen each other until a few months ago."

"I hadn't forgotten him, and it seems Meyer hadn't forgotten me either." I took his hand.

"Well, I'll be. Are the two of you together now?"

Meyer nodded slowly and then turned more forward, still holding my hand. "Once I pulled my head out of my butt and realized what I'd lost, I also knew I didn't want to let him go again."

He seemed to finally relax a little. "There has been someone on the set stirring up drama, and once I figured some things out and Luke decided that I was worth taking a chance on again, I thought it best to be straight—if you'll pardon the pun—with the world."

The audience laughed, and some of the tension that had been building seemed to dissipate.

"Meyer is an amazing man and an incredible chef—"

"And I thought cooking was going to be enough for me." Meyer turned to me. "It wasn't." He smiled, and we looked at Marla.

"He can still cook better than anyone I've ever met." I realized just what I'd said and how I'd said it. The audience tittered, and I blushed. "And I mean that in every way possible. He's hot in and out of the kitchen." I was finally starting to feel a little more comfortable.

"And Luke has an incredible blog."

"How many of you have read it?" Marla asked, and a number of hands went up before the audience broke into applause. "I have to admit that I hate bananas too."

"They're the devil's fruit," I chimed in before getting serious. "We all have food issues, and I just decided to start talking about mine."

"Does this season of *Cooking Masters* revolve around the foods you don't like?" Marla asked.

I shivered visibly, and a laugh went through the audience. "You're all going to have to tune in to see, but this season is going to be amazing. After all, Meyer is on it, and you might even get to see him cook. Though I can't give anything away." I squeezed Meyer's hand, and he turned to me.

Without thinking, I leaned over to give him a gentle kiss. The audience roared, and the applause was deafening, or it might have been, but I barely heard it. Meyer was right there in front of me, his gaze locked to mine, and that was all that mattered. When he pulled away, Marla was fanning herself.

"Okay, boys. It's hot enough in here," she chided with a smile. "Have you decided what's next for you after *Cooking Masters*?"

"Luke and I are still figuring a few things out, but I have every confidence that we will. I finally found him again, and I don't intend to let him go." Meyer's smile was radiant.

Marla stood, and Meyer and I did the same. "I want to thank both of you for coming on the show today. You're an amazing couple, and I wish you both well on this season of *Cooking Masters*." She kissed each of us on the cheek as the audience applauded, and we then exited the stage. Once we were back in the green room, I hugged Meyer and grinned.

"We did it. *You* did it," I whispered, ignoring the few others in the room.

Meyer kissed me, harder this time. "I love you, Luke. I don't know if I've told you that, but I do, and I intend to make sure that I show you just how much every day." He held me tightly once again. "I think you and I can go back to the set now. Ethan is probably going out of his mind with only Rachel around. She's been unbearable."

"Yup. Let's go." I took Meyer by the hand, and we headed out to where Felix was waiting at the car. I told him how things went after we climbed inside, and he fought rush-hour traffic all the way back to the studio.

Ethan paused shooting when the interview aired. The chefs seemed pleased for us, and so did most of the crew. The one person who stayed back, stewing, was Rachel, which was expected, I guess. We had stolen her thunder, and now all she had was her bitterness and most likely unemployment.

"God, I can't believe they bought that crap," Rachel muttered as she stormed toward the door of the viewing room. "Don't we have an episode to finish?" she practically screeched, and I shook my head.

"That's not the way to endear yourself to the people who will decide your future."

"Didn't you hear?" Justin asked. "The producers officially gave her the ax. This is her last season with the show, so she's going to be a witch from hell until this is over. Ethan did warn her that he would figure a way to write her out of the show." Justin turned away. "He threatened to tell the audience she had a case of cholera or something." He chuckled, and I couldn't help doing the same. She had been helpful and nice when I arrived, and I hated to see what was happening to her. It was like Rachel was falling apart in front of our eyes.

"I guess."

"There's better news, but I need to let him tell you or he'll have my nuts." Justin hurried away, and I watched him, wondering again if he was behind the notes and the drama, and what he expected to get out of it.

"Let's finish this episode," Meyer said, and we returned to the set with smiles on our faces.

"IT'S BEEN amazing," I told Clare on the phone after we had reviewed everything for the blog.

"I saw the interview, and I have to say, I never thought he would do it." She was as serious as a heart attack. "I didn't think he had it in him, and look now. He actually came out, talking about the show, and social media is aflutter about you two. It's almost all positive, and believe it or not, we've started to get emails and messages of support through the blog. One reader even said that you and Meyer make an adorable couple and that her son saw the interview and turned to her to tell her that he was gay." Clare choked up a little, and I felt the same tickle in my throat. "Meyer finally grew a set."

"That's a little harsh." But probably held a ring of truth.

"Have you decided what you're going to do once the show is over? I saw that you were still deciding. There isn't a lot here for you, and I could still help you if you want to relocate."

"Are you trying to get rid of me?"

"Nope. But you're happy. I can hear that. How is the show going? Are you almost done?"

"We're getting there. The competition is heating up, and things are getting—" I cut myself off. I wasn't going to talk about any of the drama on the set, which had ramped up every single damn day.

"Get off the phone—we're waiting on you," Rachel snapped as she passed.

I rolled my eyes. "I need to go, but I'll call you soon." I ended the call and followed Ms. Openly Hostile to the judging, which was painful.

"I disagree," Rachel said after Meyer expressed his opinion. Then I expressed mine, and she argued. The guest judge looked at all three of us as though we had grown two heads each, and clammed up, probably afraid to say anything in case she came after him.

"What do you think, Greg?" Meyer asked gently, after a glare at Rachel.

Greg finally expressed his opinion, which coincided with Meyer's and mine. That sent Rachel into yet another pout, but at least we had a decision. Ethan seemed relieved, and after filming the final awards and elimination, we wrapped for the night.

"God, that sucked," Meyer whispered.

I shook Greg's hand and thanked him for coming. I wanted to apologize for Rachel's behavior, because it wasn't directed at him. She was angry at Meyer and me because we had been asked to return for the next season. I thought the producers should have kept their decisions to themselves until after this season was over, but they hadn't agreed, and now it was open hostility. The only time it abated was when the chefs were present. At other times, it was all-out war on her part. What a minefield this was turning out to be.

Meyer thanked Greg as well, as Rachel stormed off.

"I need to talk to Ethan. Do you want to meet at the house?"

"Okay. But I need to stop at home and get Rosco. I'm not bringing him here any longer because of what happened to the trailer." Hell, I was scared to spend any time in the thing. If someone was after me, then that was a target. Let Rachel take her venom out wherever she wanted, but I wasn't going to put Rosco in the line of fire.

"We can go to your apartment."

"Well, actually, I was going to ask if maybe I didn't need the apartment any longer. It's going to be just a few weeks, and then…." God, I was so nervous.

"Great idea. I'll tell Ethan, and we can move your things to the house tonight. You can ride in with me in the mornings if you'd like."

"No. Felix will drive us." I stepped closer. "I'm not going to put him out of work, and the studio promised me a driver in the contract." I grinned. "I like Felix. He's a great guy, and he has a son with special needs."

Meyer patted my shoulder. "Then we'll ride in with Felix." He pulled away and headed toward the office.

I wasn't sure what to do with my time at the moment and headed to the trailer just in time to see Justin coming out.

"I put the new schedule on the table," Justin explained as he passed me. "I relocked the door on my way out."

I tried not to skip a step as the fact that Justin had keys dawned on me. Great, another thing to be afraid of. Had he had keys all the time, or had he gotten a set recently? Either way, I wasn't exactly comfortable. I checked out the trailer and got the schedule, then found a quiet spot in the shade and breeze to read. Being cooped up was the last thing I wanted.

People hurried from place to place as I sat in the grass out in front of the production office. It was bustling, but no one paid me any attention. I reviewed the schedule and checked for hidden notes, relieved that there weren't any.

After a while, I looked at my watch, because Meyer had been gone longer than I'd expected. The sun was setting, and I thought of calling Felix, but Meyer had said that he would come with me to help me gather my things. I stood and went inside. The office was quiet, and I rapped gently on Ethan's door.

"When did Meyer leave?" I asked when he called for me to come in.

"Ten minutes ago," Ethan answered. "He said there was something on the set that he needed."

"Thanks." I closed the door and hurried to the largely dark set, wondering where Meyer could be.

"I've had it with you and your little boyfriend. No one is going to replace me and get away with it."

The venom in Rachel's voice reverberated off the walls and filled me with dread. I walked slowly, trying desperately to make it across to the judging area where her voice originated. There was just enough light spilling in for me to see the big things, but I was scared and my legs shook as I drew closer.

"We had nothing to do with you leaving." The fear in Meyer's voice ran up my back like ice water. "And hurting me isn't going to get your job back."

"No, it isn't. But no one paid any attention to the damned notes, and the two of you carried on like rabbits for weeks. And just when I had the proof… someone…."

The slap of metal on metal made me jump, and I moved faster.

"You were behind the notes?" Meyer said as I reached the dark area just out of the beam of light from the doorway. Rachel sat behind the desk with a gun pointed at Meyer.

"Of course I was. I even sent one to myself and had your little boyfriend find it. That was brilliant. He's been looking at everyone on the crew with suspicion for weeks, and it was all I could do to keep from laughing at him." She waved the gun and stood. "Oh, don't worry. I'm not going to kill you." She lowered the barrel of the gun toward Meyer's legs. "But I do intend to make sure you and little Luke don't take over for me next year."

"What did we ever do to you?" Meyer asked, his hands in the air. I looked around to see if there was some sort of weapon, but I was a terrible aim with a soup pot. The chefs brought their own knives, so there were none in the kitchen that I could see.

"Come on. You both knew that I was going to be replaced, and you wormed your way in so easily. The producers were on the fence until you and your little gay geisha squeeze showed up. He cracked a damn joke about his cat, and I was Fancy Feast, just like that." She slowly walked around the desk.

Man, I had read her all wrong this whole time. I'd thought she was my friend, but it was all an act. Rachel was one cold person. She had a gun on Meyer and, damn it all, she could shoot away the person I loved and who had just professed to love me. This witch was not going to take away the happiness that I had just found. No fucking way in hell.

"No. We were never told, not until today." Meyer took a step back and pretty much disappeared from my line of sight.

I had to do something, because Rachel was unpredictable as hell. I moved away and found a rack of pots. I also found some kitchen string on one of the pantry shelves and tied one end to the top of the rack. I hoped to hell it held. Then I unwound it until I was back near the door and could see Rachel pacing like a caged tiger, front and back, nervously. I waited until she was closest to me and had turned around before pulling the string as hard as I could.

The clatter was deafening, and Rachel jumped and then bolted for the door. As soon as she approached, I leapt with everything I had and tackled her to the ground. She rolled and the gun went off, the sound nearly deafening me. I grabbed her hand and banged it on the floor until the gun clattered away, then held her down so she couldn't move.

"Are you okay?" I breathed, lifting my gaze to Meyer.

"Yes. She didn't hurt me." He hurried over and kicked the gun farther away. "But…." He gasped, and I looked down.

I was covered in red, and damn, I did a quick inventory, but felt no wounds. "I think I'm okay." I didn't want to get up to see if she was hurt. "Turn on all the lights so we can see." I kept her still, not really caring if Rachel had shot herself. The light came up, and soon the room filled with people, with Ethan leading the rescue party.

"Do you need an ambulance?" Ethan asked.

I shook my head, my gaze falling to a large can of tomatoes, the only casualty, the remains of which were all over me. "It's tomato sauce," I explained, and breathed a sigh of relief. "You stay where you are," I told Rachel when she tried to get up, swearing and cursing, but I didn't care.

"I called the police—they're on their way," Ethan said.

I stayed where I was until security arrived and took charge of the situation. When I stepped away, Meyer wrapped me in his arms. We both shook for a few seconds as the impact of what could have happened broke over us.

"Oh God. I don't understand what she hoped to gain," I whispered to Meyer.

"I think she just wanted to spread the hurt around and couldn't see any future beyond the show."

"That's true. After her little dabble with a contestant, no one was going to hire her again. That must have been the last straw, and she just sort of snapped," Ethan said.

"Yeah," I agreed. "The news revelation sure knocked her legs out from under her. She tried to disgrace us and ended up hurting herself." If she hadn't started all of this, then her secret would have remained that way and everything would have been fine. But she had to try to take matters into her own hands, and the only one who was truly hurt was herself. That was a little irony if I ever saw any.

The police arrived and peppered us with questions about everything that had happened. Thankfully, I was allowed to go clean up and change and then talk to the police. Once that was over, Ethan called us into his office for a discussion on how we were going to handle the rest of the season without Rachel. It seemed grass didn't grow under anyone's feet here in Hollywood.

"I'm going to work with the network to get another host for the season. I think we'll need someone with some experience, and they can probably recommend someone who can step in," Ethan explained. "The producers are in shock about all of this, but they agree that we need to move forward."

I nodded and so did Meyer. "We only have three episodes to go."

"Yes. There is no way we will be able to keep what happened out of the press. And we can't start retaping the season from the beginning." Ethan fidgeted as his nerves grew edgier. I just wanted to go home and try to get some sleep and get my head wrapped around all this. Meyer had to be in some state of shock, but the show would go on.

I leaned forward. "Can I make a suggestion? Can we take a few days' break from shooting? Let everyone digest what happened. If you want, Meyer and I can handle the hosting duties between us. You've done episodes when Rachel wasn't in them before, and between us we can probably handle it."

"The producers are trying to figure out how to explain this."

I shrugged. "I think on the actual show, we say nothing. The chefs aren't going to ask, and we can explain to them that we want the show to be about them and their food and not Rachel and what happened. It's less than ideal, but let's keep the show's focus on the food where it belongs and not on the antics that happened backstage." I yawned. "I'm sorry, but I don't have anything else in me today." I took Meyer's hand. "We can try to help any way we can in the morning."

"All right... I...," Ethan answered quickly, his words coming in short, nervous clips.

"You go home too. Get some rest. None of this is your fault, and you'll be able to think better in the morning." If he grew any more nervous, I was afraid Ethan was going to fly into a million pieces.

"Yeah. I think you're right." He pushed back from behind his desk and stood.

I got to my feet as well and half coaxed Meyer to his. I took a second to text Felix and ask him to pick us up, and I apologized for being so late. He messaged that he was on his way, and I was surprised to find part of the seat occupied when I slid into the car.

"This is Louis. My mother had to go to Bakersfield to visit my aunt."

I smiled and sat next to his booster seat. "I'm Luke, and this is Meyer," I said.

"Daddy drives you?" Louis asked. "You must be important to have a driver like Daddy."

I wasn't so sure about that. "I think it's because I'm not from here and I need help finding my way."

"Are you a chef?" Louis asked as Meyer closed the door.

"Louis, remember what I told you about sitting quietly for me," Felix said.

"It's okay, Felix," I told him. "I'm not a chef, but Meyer is. He's a really good one." I turned to smile at Meyer. "He makes the best food."

"Can he make tamales? Abuela makes good ones, most of the time."

"Louis," Felix said. "You know how Abuela would feel if she heard you."

He rolled his eyes the way only a kid could. "I know, but sometimes I want macaroni and cheese." He crossed his arms over his chest. "And last time her tamales were stinky." He held his nose, and I couldn't help laughing.

"I don't make stinky tamales, but I do make lots of mac and cheese. Fancy kinds too," Meyer said, leaning forward so he could

163

see Louis around me. "And my tamales and enchiladas might give your grandmother's a run for their money." He leaned over a little farther. "But don't tell her that." Meyer winked, and Louis nodded as though he'd been entrusted with an important secret.

"Daddy, I'm hungry," Louis pronounced.

"I know. We'll get dinner once I drop off Mr. Luke and Mr. Meyer."

I leaned forward. "Actually, neither of us has eaten, and it's been a lousy day." I tried not to sigh. "If you want to pull into an In-N-Out, that would be awesome."

"Daddy!" Louis bounced a little in his seat. The braces on his legs certainly didn't seem to hold Louis back.

"Are you sure it's okay?" Felix asked.

"You bet." I settled next to Meyer, taking his hand, pleased that Louis's excitement dispelled some of the pall of the day. "Sometimes we all need a good burger and shake."

"And french fries and chicken nuggets," Louis added.

I leaned toward him. "You can have whatever you want." I bet Rosco would have liked meeting Louis. Heck, he'd probably have ridden on his lap. I got a piece of paper out of my bag and wrote down the order for Meyer, Louis, and me, then handed it up to Felix, along with the money. "And get what you want." I used my best "don't argue with me" voice.

"But we need to wait until we get home to eat," Felix cautioned.

"Why don't you and Louis come up and eat with us? The food will get cold otherwise, and Louis can meet Rosco." I turned to Louis. "I have a cat, and he loves attention."

"Daddy!" Louis squealed, and I knew Felix didn't stand a chance.

"Okay. But you have to be on your best behavior, and then we're going home. You'll have to go right to bed when we get home because you have school tomorrow and Abuela will be mad if you don't get up in the morning."

"I will, Daddy," Louis promised, but somehow I figured he was going to be too wound up to actually sleep. "Is Mr. Luke a movie star?"

"I judge a cooking contest on TV," I told him. "I'm also a graphic designer. I help people with their web pages and things like that." I figured I'd leave out the blogging stuff. "I'm never going to be a movie star."

Louis shrugged. "That's okay. I'm not going to be a movie star either. They don't put kids with metal legs in the movies." He said it as though it was a fact.

"Do you want to be in the movies? I bet you could do it, metal legs or not." I had to smile, because regardless of what he said, Louis's grin never faltered. It was like he knew what his world was and was happy in it. What most of us wouldn't give for that feeling.

"I can?" He seemed entranced.

"Of course you can. You can do anything you want to." I patted his arm. "Right, Meyer?"

Meyer leaned forward. "When I was your age, I wanted to help my mom in the kitchen. My dad didn't like it because he said kitchen work was for women. My dad is kind of old-fashioned and maybe a little stupid." I had never heard Meyer say anything against his family. He had always just accepted them before.

"I help Abuela all the time," Louis said. "I like to cook. It's fun."

"That's what I thought too. So I grew up to be a chef, and I'm on TV and I have four restaurants." Meyer nudged my shoulder. "That we need to visit just as soon as the show is over."

I nodded my agreement.

"I love to cook. So don't let anyone tell you what you can't do, because you can do anything."

"I wanna be a chef, Daddy," Louis pronounced.

"Mr. Meyer is right. You can be anything you want."

Dang, I thought I might have heard a hitch in Felix's voice. He turned into the drive-through and placed the order, then pulled up, got all the food, and handed the bag into the back seat. I gave

Louis his order of french fries, and he giggled when I put my finger to my lips.

"You can't make a mess, or you'll get me in trouble with your daddy." I winked and heard Felix chuckle. Louis ate with a grin on his lips, finishing the entire order before we pulled up to the building.

After Felix parked, I carried in the food and my bag, Meyer held the doors, and Louis used his forearm crutches to get into the building and up in the elevator. I didn't say anything and did my best not to meet Felix's gaze, because I figured he'd feel the need to explain, but he didn't have to.

Inside, I sat everyone at the table, and we ate like conquering hordes. When he was done, Louis played with Rosco on the sofa. Sometimes my cat acted like a damned dog, especially when he played his own version of fetch.

"He's wonderful," Meyer said we finished eating.

"Louis is my biggest mistake and the greatest joy in my life. It's why I do what I do. He deserves the best life I can get for him." Felix finished his burger and stood. The living room had grown quiet, and when I turned, Louis was asleep, his head on one of the pillows, with Rosco curled in a ball right next to him. "I should get him home."

"Thanks." I turned to Meyer. We had planned to move my things to his place, but that wasn't a huge priority at the moment. "Tomorrow Meyer is going to give me a ride home from the studio, and then I'm going to stay with him for the rest of the trip. So the following day, you can pick us both up for the studio at his house, if you don't mind."

"Of course." Felix lifted Louis, who curled his arms around his daddy's neck.

I opened the door and whispered good night as Felix carried both Louis and his crutches out.

"Thank you. You made his night."

"I'm glad." I closed the door and collapsed on the sofa. "What next?"

Meyer sat next to me. "I sure as hell don't know. Maybe the soundstage ceiling will fall in. Godzilla could rise out of the ocean and eat the city. You and I could become parents." He laughed, and I sat back.

"Have you ever thought about having kids?" I asked, and Meyer stilled and nodded.

"Yeah. I want kids." He grew quiet again. "I had no idea that bitch was on the stage. I got a message that I had left some papers on the set, and when I went to get them, there she was. Scared the shit out of me." He wrapped his arms around his chest like he was hugging himself. I leaned closer, but Meyer shook his head. "She pulled a gun on me, and I thought she was going to kill me."

"When I saw you, all I could think was that I just found you again and I wasn't going to let that crazy wackadoodle take you away from me."

Meyer bent over, his head between his knees. "I nearly wet myself, I was so scared. I always thought I could do anything, and…."

Now I held him, tight.

"I was a complete chickenshit."

"You were not. I don't know if you realized I was there or not, but you kept her talking and got her on edge. She didn't know what to do, and that gave us an advantage. I was able to scare her and take her out. There was no way in hell I was going to leave you with her like that." I cradled Meyer's head and shoulders as the tension came to a boil. I didn't say anything about him falling apart in my arms. Hell, would it make me a terrible person if I said that in a way I liked it? Well, maybe not *liked*, but it warmed my heart to know that I wanted to make him feel better and that he felt comfortable enough to go to pieces in front of me. Okay, I was definitely a little off-balance myself, but I'd sit here all night holding Meyer and not move a muscle if it would help him. And the fact that he was willing to let me… that said a hell of a lot. "You were amazing today."

Meyer shook his head. "No. I held my own at best. You were the amazing one, and I love you for it." He lifted his gaze, and I kissed him, encircling his head in my arms, holding him with everything I had.

"She threatened to take what I wanted most in the world, and I couldn't let that happen. And I know that if things had been reversed, you'd have been there for me." Of that, I had no doubt. "You're mine, and I'll fight anyone who tries to take you away tooth and nail."

Meyer held me in return, and we stayed like that, just together, sitting, holding each other, until it was time for bed.

CHAPTER 11

THREE EPISODES. That was all there was left, and Rachel's departure had left Meyer and me with a lot more of the load to carry, but it seemed lighter and I found myself smiling—a lot.

"I loved having you at the house, sleeping in my bed," Meyer whispered from the wings. "Make that, in *our* bed."

"It took a long time."

"But we'll figure the rest out." I still wasn't fully convinced about relocating to the West Coast, but Meyer and I were still talking, and he even said he'd be willing to come back to Philadelphia. I wasn't even sure why I was so hesitant, but I had to make a decision. At the moment we were so busy that any decisions other than what I was going to wear and what I thought of the cauliflower puree—bleh, with a stuck-out tongue—were enough to keep me completely occupied.

After taking a few minutes to discuss the results, Meyer and I walked into the kitchen to announce the winner.

"Kylie, you made the best dish. I would eat that cauliflower again, and that's saying a lot." I smiled, and the few other chefs congratulated her. I then stood next to Meyer.

"Your challenge to get into the finals and have a chance at being named America's Cooking Master is something that has sent more chefs home than anything else," Meyer announced.

"And no, it isn't risotto," I interjected, to nervous smiles.

"We have decided that this challenge will be a baking challenge. Each of you is to bake, cool, frost, and decorate a cake suitable for a very special occasion." Meyer grew serious. "You will be judged on how exact your layers are, the smoothness of the frosting, decorating techniques, and, of course, taste. Today you will have ninety minutes to bake your cakes, and tomorrow you will have one hour to fill, ice, and decorate. The ovens will not be available tomorrow, so make sure your cake is as perfect as you can get it today." Meyer paused, and I stayed back. This was strictly Meyer's challenge. He was in charge and would oversee it. "Also, because your cakes will be used in a celebration, you must create a tasting cake for the judges. Kylie, you get to choose the flavors for your cake and filling, and no one else can use them."

She seemed to consider. "Chocolate and raspberry," she answered. A wonderful combination, and one of my all-time favorites.

"Very good. Your baking time starts now." Meyer stepped back as the chefs rushed to get their ingredients and go to work.

I watched from the wings while Meyer made the rounds, talking to each one to find out what they were doing.

"This isn't what was originally planned," I told Justin, who stood next to me. I was so relieved that he hadn't had anything to do with the notes and felt terrible for suspecting him.

"Any desserts were so lacking this season that Ethan wanted to force the issue," Justin whispered.

I nodded, watching as the chefs mixed their batters and got their pans prepared and ready to go into the oven. The smart ones made extra layers in case something went wrong. And one by one, the layers were in to bake. I noticed that a few enterprising chefs grabbed various types of chocolate and began making decorations and other things they were going to need, which set the others to doing the same. I loved how they adapted to each situation.

"Remember that however your layers go on your rack is how you are going to see them again in the morning. So you should cool your layers, and get them out of the pans and wrapped so they don't dry out."

I joined Meyer. "Twenty minutes."

The noise level rose, as did the sheer panic. All the chefs were pulling their layers out of the oven and getting them cooling. Kylie was the first to get hers out, and she let them settle for a few minutes while she got sheet pans with parchment ready. I was fascinated at what she was doing with her layers.

"Are you going to plastic-wrap your layers?" Meyer asked her.

"No." She filled a sheet tray with cake pans and covered them with parchment and a second sheet tray, then flipped the whole thing and set down the tray. She made sure the layers came out and then re-covered them with the cake pans. The inverted cake pans now covered the layers. She removed the top sheet tray and slid the sheet tray into the rack, then repeated the moves for the rest of her layers. "Don't have to."

Even I knew that was a very professional move.

The others wrapped their layers and were scrambling to get everything on the rack. One chef had to leave his hot layers in the pans because he ran out of time, and just covered it all.

"Two minutes," I said, standing next to Meyer to watch the final flurry of activity. Then time was up and everything came to a halt for the night. "We'll see you all in the morning."

The chefs filed out, the lights dimmed, and the set was quiet—until the buzzer sounded, and then the staff stepped in to put everything away and clean the set.

The cameramen had followed the chefs so they could capture their conversations in the "stew" room, and I turned to Meyer. "Why did they make the change, and what is this party that the cakes are being sent off to?"

Meyer shrugged. "It's something Ethan arranged. The guests at the party will be able to taste and vote on the cakes."

"Then why the tasting cakes?" I asked, suspicions growing.

"So we have a chance to know what we're walking into, I guess. This was all Ethan's idea, and I'm following his lead." Meyer seemed resigned to whatever was going to happen, so I went along with him. "Come on. We still have to review the schedule for tomorrow, and then we can go while they set up everything here."

"ARE YOU really sure about this?" I asked Meyer as we climbed into bed.

"That I want you here?" He smiled and pulled me down onto the king-size bed. "You betcha." Meyer laughed, happily, ringing and full of joy. "Have you spoken with Clare?"

"Yeah." I sighed. "She thinks that maybe I'm rushing into things. Not that she isn't happy for me, because she is. And she'll remain my assistant and help with the blog and things the way she always has. It isn't that. I think she's worried about how fast things have changed."

Meyer slipped under the covers and tugged me to him. "I get that. But her opinion doesn't really matter. It's yours that counts, and what you feel." He lifted my gaze with just a finger under my chin. "What are you worried about? Really?"

"That I'm going to wake up and all this is going to change again." I had to be honest.

"It isn't, and you are awake. This is real—I feel it right here." He put his hand on my chest. "You loved me when I was a real dick and a half. And what I can't believe is that you love me now." Meyer lay back on the bed, tugging me on top of him. "I want you, Luke." Meyer swallowed, and a touch of nerves filled his eyes. "I want you to make love to me."

I stilled and nearly gasped. That was something very new. Meyer had never, ever trusted me—and as far as I know, anyone—to…. I gulped. "Are you sure?"

"Yes, Luke. I want you to be the first." He was so earnest, and I threw my arms around his neck, leaning close, my lips to his ear.

"Then I will be. But not tonight. Just the idea that you asked is enough." Meyer was not a receiving kind of guy. He was a pitcher through and through, and man, he deserved a… whatever award

172

they give for pitchers… in the bedroom. I could have tried to think of what they called it, but my mind and soon the rest of me was occupied—very occupied, and not with that particular type of balls.

"TEN MINUTES," I called as the remaining chefs put the finishing touches on their cakes. One had used fondant, and I was wondering what it was going to taste like. The cake was attractive enough, but fondant tasted pretty sweet.

Meyer and I spoke about some of our observations so they could be edited in later, and then time was up. Each chef stood at their station with their cake in front of them. The buzzer sounded to note that we were clear, and I sighed as the staff hurried in.

The cakes were all boxed for transport, and then Ethan gave the order for Meyer and me to go. Felix waited outside, and he drove us across town to Santa Monica and a beachside restaurant with a large deck that overlooked the ocean, the chefs, their cakes, and the camera people all following.

"Something is going on," I told Meyer.

"Just play along," Meyer said as a number of people filed in.

Meyer stood in front of the camera, smiling. "Welcome, everyone, to Kilcrease in Santa Monica. We want to thank them for hosting us this afternoon. As you all know, our chefs have created four cakes, and all they've been told is that they are for a special occasion. And that's true. But what they didn't know, until right now, is that the patrons here today are going to vote on what they believe to be the best cake. The winner will receive an express trip to the finale and ten thousand dollars, and one chef will be eliminated."

"What's the occasion?" I asked, half forgetting that we were taping.

Meyer grinned. "Luke and I have been judging this contest all season, but along the way, something else happened."

I gasped.

"See, when we both agreed to be part of this season of *Cooking Masters*, neither of us knew that the other was going to be here." Meyer's smile slipped away. "I fell in love with Luke years ago, but was too afraid to see it through. Fate, in the form of *Cooking Masters*, stepped in and brought Luke back to me."

I put my hand over my mouth, and Meyer put an arm around my shoulders.

"Don't worry. I am not going to ask you to marry me here on camera. Something like that should be done properly, over a fine dinner, cooked by an amazing chef, like any of our contestants… or me."

I shook my head and rolled my eyes, the cameras capturing it all, I'm sure.

"So here's why we're here. Luke Walker, will you stay here in Los Angeles with me, share my life, and make me the happiest man on earth?"

"That sounds an awful lot like a proposal," I warned him.

"Let me finish, because this is the important part. Will you host the next season of *Cooking Masters* with me?"

I nodded, grinned, and burst into laughter. It was so cheesy and funny and brilliant that I couldn't possibly say no. "Yes. I will do all of those things, for as long as you—and the producers—will let me."

EPILOGUE

"I AM not going to do yet another post on mushrooms," I told Clare over the phone. "But I will do one on organ meats, because those are yucky to a degree I never thought possible." I shuddered. "I'll get it to you so you can add it to the blog by tomorrow. Get pictures of things like liver, brains, and kidneys for it. Preferably cooked, because I don't want any more raw meat comments."

She chuckled. "Okay. I can take care of that. Are you going to do a tease about the next season? You really should. Every reader knows that shooting is going to start soon, and they want some of the inside scoop."

"I spoke with the producers, and they said as long as I run the posts through them first." I knew exactly what she was going to say. "They aren't being dicks about it. They only need to be sure that nothing secret or important to the outcome of the show is included." I understood their concern and had offered them the choice to review the posts. I was well aware that I had to be careful. "What I want to do is time the post about each episode so that it hits the blog a few days before the episode airs. It will help drive up interest in the show." I checked my watch. "I need to go."

"You're nervous about something." Sometimes I swore she had phone intuition.

"Yeah. Meyer and I are having dinner tonight with his mom and dad. They arranged to come to the city and asked to have dinner with him. Meyer told them that the two of us would be happy to have dinner, and he said they agreed." I was finding it hard to believe, but then, if they were willing to meet Meyer halfway, I could be there for Meyer.

"Holy shit!" Clare swore. "That's like—"

"I know. Like a blizzard just struck LA." I thought the two events were equally likely. "Anyway, I need to go get dressed and find something… butch to wear." I snickered.

"So those paper-thin workout shorts are out."

"I was thinking a pair of jeans and a ripped T-shirt, but I'm being nice. Just a proper light blue shirt and dark dress pants. With a rainbow pocket square for a little color." I had to tease her—it was so much fun.

"Har-har. Go on. I'll talk to you once you send the post."

I ended the call and left the office, finding Meyer pacing the living room, already dressed. "I'm going to change. I'll be just a minute." I kissed him and then went into the bedroom to put on the clothes I'd laid out earlier. Then I grabbed a fresh shirt from Meyer's closet and carried it to the living room.

"What's that for?" Meyer asked, pausing his pacing.

"You already sweated through the one you're wearing. Put this on and try to relax. We can go once you do." I waited while he changed shirts, and then we left the house. I drove us to his restaurant just off downtown as Meyer stewed in his own juices, almost literally. I parked in Meyer's spot, and we got out.

"We're early."

"It looks like your mom and dad are too." It could only be them. His dad looked a lot like Meyer—the same facial shape and cheekbones. Meyer had his mother's eyes and hair. My nerves went through the roof as I thought about what could possibly happen and how this entire idea could completely crash and burn. This was a huge step for Meyer and for us. Up until now, his mom and dad had shown little interest in meeting me at all. I really expected that there would be some part of Meyer that would always be conflicted over his relationship with me and the one with his parents. "Go on over, say hello, and take it from there," I told him.

Meyer's mother gripped her purse handle with both hands, and it was clear his parents were as nervous as we were.

176

Meyer nodded, closing his car door and walking to where they stood just outside the restaurant door. I followed, and at first the three of them just looked at one another. It was awkward, stiff, and really weird. Then his mother pulled a tissue out of her purse and wiped her eyes before hugging Meyer. She was crying, and I was willing to bet he was too. Meyer hugged his dad before stepping back.

"Luke, this is my mom and dad, Richard and Joselle." He seemed to breathe for the first time since he'd gotten their call. Hell, my heart finally started beating again.

"It's good to meet you both." I shook their hands and motioned toward the door. "Meyer has a table reserved for us." Standing out here looking at one another, wondering what we had to say, wasn't making anyone feel any more at ease.

"Wonderful." His mother wiped her eyes and took Meyer's arm, heading toward the restaurant. I followed with Meyer's dad.

"We saw you with Meyer on the show," Richard said a little tentatively. "We watched every episode."

I nodded, understanding what he was saying.

"It was…"

I braced for what was to follow.

"…startling how happy Meyer was." He turned his attention forward to where Meyer and his mother were talking. And I breathed deeply, trying not to sigh. That was the last thing I had expected him to say, and it must have taken a great deal of effort on his part.

"I love seeing him happy." And I did. Meyer and his parents might never truly understand each other, but this was a step forward for all of them.

At the steps, Meyer held back, and his mom and dad went up together with the two of us following.

"Do you think it will be okay?"

"I hope so. There's a lot of water under the bridge."

177

"True." I turned to him, pausing on the steps. "But think about it—our story is one of second chances." I turned to his parents, and Meyer did as well. "And sometimes they're the best ones of all." I slipped my arm around Meyer's waist and we headed upward… together.

ANDREW GREY is the author of more than one hundred works of Contemporary Gay Romantic fiction. After twenty-seven years in corporate America, he has now settled down in Central Pennsylvania with his husband, Dominic, and his laptop. An interesting ménage. Andrew grew up in western Michigan with a father who loved to tell stories and a mother who loved to read them. Since then he has lived throughout the country and traveled throughout the world. He is a recipient of the RWA Centennial Award, has a master's degree from the University of Wisconsin–Milwaukee, and now writes full-time. Andrew's hobbies include collecting antiques, gardening, and leaving his dirty dishes anywhere but in the sink (particularly when writing). He considers himself blessed with an accepting family, fantastic friends, and the world's most supportive and loving partner. Andrew currently lives in beautiful, historic Carlisle, Pennsylvania.

Email: andrewgrey@comcast.net
Website: www.andrewgreybooks.com

ANDREW GREY

BORROWED
Heart ♥

Robin, the recipient of a brand-new heart, knows he can't give it to just anyone....

Robin's been through his share of upsets recently, from heart transplant surgery to a brutal breakup. But his experiences have taught him life is short, and he's ready to seize the day and start anew. A job at Euro Pride Tours is just the kind of adventure he's looking for. He gets to see the world and live a little, but love isn't on his radar screen. He isn't sure his heart can endure that again.

Johan might've disappointed his family by striking out on his own, but when he meets Robin, he has no intention of letting him down. Each man is just what the other needs to feel whole again, and while Johan might not be the man Robin originally thought he was, he's exactly what the doctor ordered to make Robin's borrowed heart beat faster. As the tour through Germany progresses, they grow closer, but when Robin's ex joins the tour, he could bring their blossoming love to a dramatic halt.

www.dreampsinnerpress.com

Martin Graham built his business from the ground up with hard work and intuition. Due to a degenerative eye disease, he's learned to rely on his other senses to feel out the competition. To realize his dream, he just needs to broker one last deal… and finally secure an assistant.

Brock Littleton is desperate for money—desperate enough take the job no one else wants: assistant to demanding, fussy, intensely private Mr. Graham.

Everything about Brock gets under Martin's skin in ways he never expected, making him realize a successful business isn't the only component to a happy future. But as Martin's deal comes together, one of the prices could be the relationship with Brock that Martin is just starting to believe could be real.

www.dreamspinnerpress.com

ANDREW GREY

PULLING STRINGS

A high-stakes case of industrial espionage ties them together, but before they can pursue their attraction, they must find out who's pulling the strings.

Devon Donaldson doesn't know how a folio of stolen corporate secrets found its way into his bag, and certainly can't think of anyone who'd want to frame him. The trouble is, he has to convince Powers McPherson.

Devon's firm hired Powers to investigate the theft of a new banking system, and so far Devon is his only lead. While Powers's gut tells him Devon is innocent, he has no intention of letting Devon out of his sight… for more than one reason. Working together to get Devon's life back leads to feelings far beyond cooperation. But before they can act on them, they need to find the group of thieves intent on ruining Devon's reputation.

www.dreamspinnerpress.com

Reunited

CURSED · DREAMSPINNER PRESS

Andrew Grey

Back in high school, nobody noticed quiet nerd Kevin Howard.

But everybody noticed handsome, athletic, and ultrapopular jock Clay Northrup.

They had nothing in common and lived in different worlds.

But a lot can change in fifteen years, and when they meet again at their high school reunion, Clay is no longer the big man on campus, and Kevin isn't hiding in a corner anymore.

Can they put aside who they were? Can one night really lead to forever?

www.dreamspinnerpress.com

ANDREW GREY

SURVIVE

AND CONQUER

Newton DeSantis was on the ground when the towers collapsed on 9/11. Though he still carries the scars on his body and his heart, he's determined to ease some of the world's suffering. Now a social worker and father to two children with special needs, he's doing his best. But when his son's health takes a drastic turn, Newton knows he can't do it alone.

Family law attorney Chase Matthews is a rising star, and he's in high demand. Still, Newton is very persuasive, and Chase takes his case pro bono. Everything about the other man appeals to Chase, but he's determined to keep the relationship professional—even though, after meeting Newton's kids, he wants to be a part of their lives.

Chase's job doesn't always allow him to pick his clients, though, and a case that could make him partner will put him on the opposite side of the courtroom from Newton—along with everything he believes in and the future they could build together.

www.dreamspinnerpress.com

Made in United States
Orlando, FL
22 March 2026

79557838R00115